Varney the Vampyr

Vampyr

Book 2: Vampyr Hunter B

Words and pictures
By
David Lowrie

VARNEY THE VAMPYR, VAMPYR HUNTER B
BY
DAVID LOWRIE

10 9 8 7 6 5 4 3 2 1
FIRST PRINTING, 2022

ISBN 9798484258796

BLACK DOG GAMEBOOKS
Blackdoggamebooks@gmail.com

Acknowledgements

Thank you to:

Jack, Emily and Daniel Furlong– who will always be my George, Flora and Henry! Thanks for enjoying the book, and walking around quoting it!

Rebecca Furlong for supporting, art critiques and generally being a lovely sister,

Howard Ellis for being my fiercest critic (in a good way)

Brian Twomey, and Daniel and Barry, for chapter by chapter reaction!

David Gotteri for proof reading and great support

James Spearing, Rob Hatton and Louise Lee for play-testing

And finally:

My wonderful family: Vanessa, Emelia and Jeannie – for supporting and encouraging me, and giving me the time to write this.

Prologue – A New Arrival

The plane was a single engine Cessna 172, privately hired out of Prague in, if not in an outright suspicious manner, then definitely by slightly shady means. On board were two people – the pilot and a passenger. It was on its final approach to Lerner airfield, a small airport in the south east of England. The radio crackled as the tower contacted the plane, call sign EME-1291. The pilot spoke to the tower and received his instructions, and then started his descent.

It was dark outside as it was about 3:30am local time, and the sun had yet to start to climb over the horizon. It was also stormy outside, and the rain lashed the small windows of the plane. The pilot struggled to make out the lit up runway, due to the torrential rain. Then a cross-wind caught the plane, and it started to shudder and jump as it entered the turbulence.

The passenger sat in his seat silent as a grave, and as still as a corpse. He did not even flinch as the plane shuddered and rolled through the air. He stared stoically ahead, unblinkingly, unseeingly, ignoring everything around him.

The pilot shouted back to him,

"Better hold on, pal, it's gonna to be a bumpy landin"

The passenger didn't reply, or even acknowledge the pilot. Then the plane touched down with a thud and a lurch, and bounced back up into the air. The pilot struggled with the stick, trying to force the plane back to the ground. The plane continued to bounce and career down the runway, closing fast on the bright lights of the small glass and steel building that served as the airport's terminal.

The pilot gritted his teeth and finally got the plane on the ground and he stuck on the brakes. The sudden deceleration forced him to lurch forward in his seat. The passenger didn't move an inch. Then the brakes screeched, as the plane hurtled towards the terminal. But the brakes held and the plane's velocity slowed. It came to rest with a lurch no more than 20 feet from the tall glass windows of the terminal.

The pilot flicked a few switches and the engine started to power down, and the internal lights flickered on. The pilot, forehead still dripping with sweat, turned around and smiled in relief at his passenger.

"Well, mate, we made it. A bit rough there for a while but any landing you can walk away from, eh?" he half joked.

His passenger did not reply, just unclipped his seatbelt and stood up. He grabbed hold of a large battered leather suitcase. It looked like it must weigh at least 30 kilos, but he picked it up as it were made of cotton wool and feathers. He walked over to the cabin door, and opened it, and kicked the fold up steps down. Then without a word, or even a look at the pilot, he climbed down the stairs onto the wet tarmac.

He strode to the terminal building and walked into the bright light. As Lerner was only a minor airport, there was very little in the way of security. There was a single passport control desk, with a conveyor belt and a metal detector arch. Behind the desk was a single customs officer, who at present was thoroughly immersed in her Sudoku puzzle book. Her ID badge gave her name as, rather unfortunately, Nora Bone. She still hadn't quite forgiven her father for that - as is often the way with dads, he wasn't half as funny as he thought he was.

The passenger walked, or more strode, over to the desk. It was a walk of intent that said "get out of my way". An implacable, unstoppable march. He stood at the desk and waited, silently. Then Nora became aware that his shadow was blocking out part of her light. She looked up and smiled, a smile of boredom and slight annoyance, as she was just about to crack a particularly frustrating puzzle.

"Passport please", she asked in a monotonous voice of pure boredom, "And please place any luggage onto the conveyer belt."

The passenger swung the case onto the belt with ease. Then he reached into an inside pocket and pulled out a worn and dog-eared passport. He passed it to the officer. Nora flicked it open and looked at it.

She looked at the face in the passport and then looked up, for almost the first time, into the face of the man in front of her. First of all she had to look up some way, as she was sat down and the man towered over her, at a good four inches over six foot tall. Her neck clicked in protest as she seemed to have to look up towards the stars.

He was both broad and slender, or so it seemed, as he was wearing a long brown leather Duster style coat that almost reached his ankles. She looked up into the face and saw it was shrouded in shadow, as he was wearing a broad brimmed hat.

"Please remove the hat" she asked, although it was really more an order, but it was always nice to ask. The man grunted, the first noise he had made, and swept the hat from his head with a quick economical movement of his hand – much faster than to be expected for a man his size.

She looked at the face. It was wide and quite finely featured. It would be seen by many to be an attractive face, if it were not set in a perpetual frown. The brows were creased, and the brown eyes seemed to squint out from under them. The nose was long and straight, apart from the part that wasn't. The mouth was wide but downturned. On top of the head was a mop of blonde brown hair that hadn't been styled, more hacked into something approximating a style with a sharp knife. A thick stubble, that was working its way into being upgraded into an actual beard, covered his cheeks and broad, pronounced chin. The stubble was slightly darker than the hair on his head, and flecked with grey in places.

Nora checked and the face matched the photo, which was wearing the exact same frown.

"Thank you Mr.,............Oh, Earthborn. Nathaniel Wardost Earthborn. Boy, that's quite a name, sir."

"Yes it is", Mr. Earthborn replied. His voice was almost a whisper, if a whisper could be dragged over course sandpaper. And then pulled along a gravel path, via a bed of razor blades. It was a voice that chilled.

Nora leafed through the pages of the passport, looking at the stamps on the pages.

"First time back in the UK for 5 years?"

"Yes."

"My, we have been around haven't we? Prague, Budapest, Reykjavik, Bucharest, Ankara, Helsinki, Tbilisi, Kiev to name but a few. Do you travel for work?"

"Yes."

"Lucky man, if I am lucky I get 2 weeks in Benidorm these days. But my other half won't go anywhere else. Likes all the English pubs, he does: the John Smith's Smooth Flow, the Premier League, and a Sunday dinner. I do say "why travel all the way there if you are just going to eat and drink what you eat and drink at home", but he won't listen. So what do you do?"

Earthborn's frown became even deeper in frustration, but he knew better than to upset customs officials. He tried to be patient – not his strongest suit. In fact, it was probably one of the things he was worst at. That and baking.

"I'm an exterminator."

"An ex-terminator? Like Arnie will be when he retires", Nora giggled to herself, proud of her witticism. Earthborn's frown deepened further still, if that was possible. The laugh died on Nora's lips.

"Sorry,what? Like a rat catcher?" Nora asked.

"Sometimes my prey may seem like rats, but I specialise in larger vermin. Much larger. Much more dangerous"

"There must be a lot of work out there?"

Earthborn placed his large hands on the desk, and leaned down towards Nora. He whispered. Given that his usual voice was little more than a whisper, then this was barely a murmur.

"There are still deep and dark places in this world, and in those dark places are vermin and parasites that need to be destroyed, no matter the cost. Few have the skill to prevail against these creatures. But beware, even here you never know what is near, watching, waiting to strike."

Nora leaned back, a bit rattled, and decided she had better move this strange man on.

"So what is the purpose of your visit to the UK?" she asked, trying to wrap up the necessary questions.

Earthborn's face looked serious and stoic. His voice was joyless as a tomb as he replied,

"Pleasure."

Chapter One – Ratpole Renovated

You know that house near you, the one at the end of the road? The one that looks a bit scary. The one you always walk by really quickly. But only walk, never run, as if you ran - he'd chase you.

But back to the house. It's an old house, set back from the road. It's thin and tall, with tall and thin windows. In the middle is a crooked green front door, paint peeling everywhere. The mortar is crumbling from between the brickwork, and the whole house smells of damp and decay. Well, it used to.

In the months since the Bannerworth children first met Sir Francis, the vampyr (rhymes with adhere - just for old times' sake) who lived at the end of the road, they had helped him make a few changes.

It was the summer holidays, and under the apparent direction of Mr. March (although in reality George was actually in charge) they had made some improvements. The green door had been sanded and re-painted a slightly different shade of green. The old piano behind it had been dusted and tuned, and was often now playing.

It turned out Sir Francis was quite an accomplished pianist. It probably helped that he had two major advantages to mortals. Firstly he was 800 odd years old - and some of those years had been very odd – and so he had plenty of time to practice.

Secondly, he had ridiculously long fingers, which seems to almost be able to stretch as if they were made from elastic. He was so good he was able to play "The Devils Ladder" by Ligeti - the third hardest thing to play on a piano. And he could play it blindfolded and with one arm tied behind his back.

But back to the house. As well as the door, the rest of the woodwork had been painted, cracked windows repaired, and even the garden gate had been oiled so it didn't creak and groan anymore. Henry was quite upset by that, as he quite liked it when it sounded scary as they opened it. The grass had been cut, although really it was more like it was hacked back as it was so long.

It's now quite sunny in the garden, and even in the day Sir Francis can sometimes be seen outside – although his one concession to the bright light is to wear a wide straw hat, so his bald pate didn't blister.

Now when there are lights at the window, it's not a flickering flame of a candle, but the bright light of halogen bulbs. Yes, the house had been re-wired. Or rather wired, as it never had any wire in the first place. And most importantly, according to the Bannerworth kids, it now had Wi-Fi.

So during the summer there are lots of comings and goings to the house.
Post is delivered.
Parcels arrive via a procession of battered white vans as Sir Francis discovers the joy of internet shopping.

But we will have to wait until the autumn to find out if anyone still dares to visit the house when trick or treating.

And whatever you do, try to avoid the cellar.

Chapter Two — Of Werewolves and Flying Squirrels

Chili squealed with delight, and scampered along the roof beam, his sharp claws gripping onto the wooden beam, his tail swishing. He was excited as the Bannerworth kids had just walked into the room – and more specifically, Flora.

The erstwhile Professor Chillingworth had changed somewhat. For the first few weeks after he had inadvertently changed into a squirrel to try to escape, he had been kept in the silver cage. Flora looked after him, feeding him daily, cleaning the cage, and making little toys for him – which he grudgingly played with as he could not overcome his animalistic instincts. As he could not change back into his new vampyric form whilst he was in his cage, he initially fumed and resented Flora. But then he started to forget about his other form and got used to his life as a squirrel. Albeit a green flying squirrel that may or may not be immortal.

What can happen with animorphs such as vampyrs and lycan, is that if they spend an extended time in their animal form, then they forget how to turn back. Or maybe forget isn't the right word. They stop wanting to change back and become used to their new forms, as their forms influence their personality.

The Professor was aware of his past life, but he really didn't care about it, and he now had no desire to change back. Over time this had become apparent and Flora, under strict agreement with the others, had been allowed to let him out of the cage.

But after a few more weeks, he now had the run of Ratpole House. He liked all the kids, but loved Flora, and was normally seen perched on her shoulder, chittering away. Flora had renamed him "Chili", which he secretly quite liked, as chilies were one of his favorite snacks. Whilst he could not talk as such, he soon developed a way of communicating with Flora via various whistles, clicks and squeaks.

Flora similarly adored Chili, and they became almost inseparable (except when Flora had to go home – she had tried to convince mum to let him stay as a pet, but Mrs. Bannerworth had initially stayed resolute. Eventually she agreed and bought him a cage for the corner of Flora's room – where he stayed over from time to time).

Chili scampered down the doorframe and dropped onto Flora's shoulder, chirping with delight. Flora laughed and ruffled his fur.

They were both almost bowled over as Mr. March ran past them. Or more like he loped, four-legged almost through them. He ran over, and jumped up at Henry, and soon they were rolling around on the floor, Henry giggling, Mr. March growling. Then they both got up and hared out of the room into the garden, where Henry found a tennis ball and kept throwing it for Mr. March to fetch.

Recently Mr. March had been spending an increasing amount of time in his other form, as a great wolf. But never too long so that he forgot to change back. He split his time between 99 Shackledown Road and Ratpole House, staying with Sir Francis when the moon was full. Even when he did turn into a wolf on these nights, the only issues locally was an increase in complaints about a dog wailing all night, and a distinct reduction in the local wild rabbit population.

When they didn't have other things to do, Henry and Mr. March spent most of their time together, normally playing silly games in the garden. Werewolves can be very loyal, and slowly Mr. March saw Henry as his own, to protect and care for.

Sir Francis did not seem to mind the subversion of his Maximus. He was kept too busy by George. The two would talk for hours, as George asked unending questions of Sir Francis. A long life had meant that Sir Francis knew a lot about a lot of things, and a little about others. They talked about history, politics, astronomy (but not astrology as George said that was silly), science, and technology. And about vampyrs and other mythical creatures, of course.

They were often found in the library, pouring over a dusty old leather book, or staring intently at a chess board as they try to outsmart and outthink each other. Sir Francis was amazed that George showed such an aptitude for the game, and was getting closer to beating him.

George, although questioning about just about everything, rarely reflected on his own emotions and feelings. However it was clear that he was becoming attached to Sir Francis as a father figure. Flora and Henry had been too young to remember that terrible night years ago when they found out about their father – but George, who was about six at the time, remembered it all too well.

So the days went by, and their strange lives fell into a normal routine. Everything seemed perfect as each of the kids had their own unique friend to occupy them. The days were long and seemingly endless (although Sir Francis often grumbled about that), and there wasn't a cloud on the horizon.

Or so they thought.

Chapter Three – the Truth is Out There

When you think of a town's library, you may imagine that it's an old Victorian style house, built of red bricks, with beautiful stone columns around the wide, heavy oak door. Inside are wide rooms with high ceilings and mahogany bookcases from floor to ceiling. The reading tables would also be oak, and have green downward facing lamps, and the atmosphere inside was always peaceful and serene.

Bedlamton Library was none of those things. It was a squat square building, split over two levels, all concrete and glass and right angles. Weather and time had given it a tired, gloomy look.

Inside, the ground floor was wide and open. The flooring was the kind of carpeting that your shoes often stuck to. It also had an annoying habit of building up static electricity so if you touched one of the metal shelves, you got a shock. The chairs were the type with metal frames and moulded plastic seats and backs. The kind that are too large for kids to sit in without their bums nearly sliding through the oddly placed hole at the back. But they were also the type that were just a bit too small for adults to fit in without them getting a trapped nerve in their leg after about 30 minutes. They were the very opposite of comfortable.

If anyone spoke above a whisper, then one of the staff would give them a cold stare. The atmosphere was not peaceful, more oppressive. Not kind, more passive aggressive.

That morning, the library was busy. It was Wednesday, market day in town, and that always brought the pensioners in by droves on the bus. As they were making a day of it, they always brought their library books to return or renew in various tartan push along trolleys, or huge camping backpacks.

Behind the counter was Ms. Phlips. She had a long thin face and her brown hair was scraped back in a bun. A pair of steel rimmed glasses perched on the end of her rather long nose. She had one of those faces that made it hard to guess if she was 33 or 66. She was the library's manager, and she liked calm and order. And rules – she loved rules.

She was busy doing one of her favourite jobs, stamping the returns back into the library, when she heard someone clearing his throat. She looked up and saw a man, leaning (more slouching – and Ms. Phlips didn't like slouching) on the counter. She stared over the top of her glasses and assessed the man.

He was middle aged and middling in height. Everything about him seemed middling. His hair was a dull red, which seemed to be scraped over from one temple to the other. It was the sort of hairstyle that doesn't enjoy a windy day. His face was round, and he wore a pair of tinted glasses (the sort that would change tint if they were out in the sun – the kind that were popular when your parents were young). At the moment the lenses were light yellow. He had a thin moustache that crawled along his top lip, and a rather poor attempt at a goatee on his chin.

He was wearing a grey hiker's jacket. Waterproof and practical with lots of pockets. The sort you would get from a high street outdoor sports retailer that always had 30% off everything. On its lapels were various badges and patches – CAMRA, CND, and one that said "I am X".

Under that was a black t-shirt, with letters in large white type across it. The kind of t-shirt that was cool for about 30 minutes in the 80's. It was about two sizes too small for him, and only just covered his notable paunch.

What the t-shirt said wasn't clear due to the jacket, and the Pentax ME Super 35mm camera that was hung around his neck. Across his chest was slung a messenger style bag. Ms. Phlips couldn't see his legs, but she guessed he was the type of man who favoured corduroy trousers. And he did – brown ones no less. But they were so practical, he would no doubt tell you at length, as if you get stuck outside in a storm, they didn't absorb water like jeans. On his feet, she thought, were probably a pair of garish luminous coloured trainers, which no one north of 25 should ever try to wear. Again, she was right. Ms. Phlips was a good judge of character.

"Excuse me, my good lady", he said in a distinctly nasal voice "Please allow me to show you my credentials."

And with that one podgy hand flew up. A black leather wallet was between his chubby fingers, the kind the FBI like to use. He flipped it open, and in it was a photo ID and a metal badge (that looked like it had been ordered from eBay or was found at the bottom of a breakfast cereal box). Ms. Phlips plucked it from his hand and looked down at it.

"Ray Tuesday, PPI? What's a PPI? Payment Protection Insurance? Look if you are selling insurance then I don't need any thank you very much, and I am much too busy with work."

"No, it's P.P.I.", replied Tuesday. He said it like there were full stops between each letter. "I am the country's pre-eminent Paranormal Private Investigator."

"Shouldn't that be P.P.P.I. then?" snapped back Ms. Phlips, making sure she exaggerated the full stops. "And is there much competition in your field?"

"Well, we are a select few. A rare band of searchers for the truth. Crusaders for freedom and free speech."

"So no then? Just you isn't it?"

"Not at all madam. There's me and, well, one other. But he is just a hack compared to me."

"If you say so, Mr.......Tuesday. Now, others are waiting and so how can I help you?"

"Very good. Can you tell me where your archives are? I need to do some research. Land registry, titles and deeds. That sort of thing"

"If you log on to any of the computers, sir, it is all on-line"

Tuesday bristled a bit. He didn't like the internet much. Or rather he didn't trust it. He liked it as he could broadcast his pod-casts, upload his findings to social media, and buy cheap fake ID badges. However he didn't trust, by his estimation, 97.4% of the content on the net – as it was all controlled by the government. Which government he wasn't exactly sure. And the majority of the remaining 2.6% was just rubbish.

"No, records can be changed and altered on the internet. I want the original paper versions."

"As you wish, but it will take time. The archives are down the bottom, turn left."

"Thank you, madam, you have been *mostly* helpful", he smirked, and before Ms. Phlips could respond, he turned dramatically on his heels and walked off. Or rather he would have done if his messenger bag hadn't swung out and knocked over a stack of books.

Muttering to himself, and annoyed that he didn't get to flounce out with the last word, he bent down and stacked them back up. Ms. Phlips just smiled thinly at him, taking the high-ground and the moral high-ground both at once, as he scrambled around on the dirty floor. He huffed, stood up and walked off.

He reached the bottom of the room and turned left, walked into a brick wall, and then went back and turned the other left (the right left). He sometimes forgot little things like directions. He went through a doorway into a new room. Or rather it was new to him, but it was in fact a very old room.

The walls were crammed with old metal shelves, which were in turn crammed with old books, files and parchments. The overall smell of the room was of dust and old paper. There were old wooden desks in the centre (but still no green lamps). A handful were occupied, mostly by older men or women, pouring over birth, death and marriage certificates as they tried to research their family tree.

No-one in the room was in fact related to royalty, as they had hoped after watching that programme on the BBC. The closest to famous the occupants of the room had were more infamous- as Mr. Catchhead was distantly related to Jack Ketch. Ketch was the head executioner (and therefore also body executioner) for Charles II, and was famous for being inept with his axe when he turned the Duke of Monmouth's head into a toast-rack.

Tuesday walked to the enquiries desk at the end. A man in his 60's or from the 60's, one of the two, was behind it. He was reading an old book and making notes in a small black notebook.

Tuesday walked up and cleared his throat. For long moments the man didn't react, and then slowly he looked up and nodded.

"Yessir?" it seemed to be a greeting and a question all rolled into one.

"I would like to examine some documentation. I have been hired by some people of import to do this vital work, and so I expect your full co-operation."

The man, whose ID badge showed a rather shocked photo of the wearer, and the name John Twentyman, shrugged.

"Whatdoyou want then?" he asked, clearly not impressed by Tuesday's tone.

"First of all, how far do these records go back?"

"Back to 1086 and the Doomsday Book, sir. Bedlamton was mentioned in the book as being established in 1067 by Master William Hubert..........."

"That's is enough, I do not need a history lesson. Tempus fugit my good man. Do you know what that means?"

"Time flies." Twentyman replied.

"No you obviously don't well, it's from the Latin, and it means "time".....wait a minute what did you just say?"

"Time flies."

"Hmm, so you know Latin? Educated man", Tuesday muttered to himself frustrated.

"Nah, I just remember it from an old X-Files episode."

Tuesday was really annoyed now, as in truth that's the only way he knew it as well.

"Be that as it may, can you point me in the direction of the birth and death certificates, precisely those relating to names beginning with "V"?"

Twentyman pointed, "Shelf 18, Row 3, about a third of the way down."

"Most excellent. And now title deeds to properties?"

"Yes, we got those as well. Which ones?"

"Well that related to Shackelton Road, and, more specifically, number 99 and a property called Ratpole House."

"This way sir."

Chapter Four – A Convoluted Journey

Earthborn arrived in Bedlamton at about 7:17pm on the evening of Wednesday 25th July. He retraced his steps in his mind.

Back at Lerner airport, after he had been questioned by Miss Bone, then they had checked his baggage. The X-ray machine on the conveyor belt was a bit of a problem, as the case was too big to fit through the arch. So instead it had to be a manual inspection. No! Not that sort.

He placed the case on a table.

"Open it, please" asked, or more precisely, ordered Miss Bone.

He reached down and turned the dials on the old combination lock to the numbers 777, and turned the catches horizontal, and clicked it. The lock hasps sprung out and he threw the lid back. Inside was just clothes, a pair of boots and a washbag. Bone rummaged through it and found nothing of interest. Half frustrated, as there was something off about this man; and half relieved, as she felt uneasy in his presence, she slammed it shut.

"OK you are good to go, Mr. Earthborn. Apologies for the inconvenience" she said rather insincerely.

Earthborn clicked the locks closed, turned the catches back vertical, and scrambled the numbers on the two dials. He grunted, and picked up his bag.

"So long" he whispered, as he stalked off into the night.

From there, he had walked 5 miles to the nearest train station, and then crisscrossed the south east of England, split up by a couple of random bus rides from station to station. In the end, he ended up hailing a taxi, and travelling the last 10 miles in the cab to his ultimate destination.

All the time he had watched in the crowds to see if any face was replicated. His enemies were clever, and would often try to catch him, but he was happy (relatively speaking – he didn't really do happy. Along with patience and baking) that he had got to his destination unseen.

He got out and paid the cabbie, who was overjoyed when he didn't get a tip, so much so that he cried out delight. He walked into the Bedlamton Arms and checked in, paying cash.

Safely in his attic room, he swung the bag onto the bed, and left the catches vertical. Then he set the two combinations as 666, and clicked the locks. The hasps sprung open. He threw back the lid and looked inside.

At first it appeared no different, just some neatly folded clothes, boots and a wash bag. But Earthborn lifted up this tray and moved it to one side. Underneath was a completely different section. The next level had a foam insert, which had been cut to hold various implements and instruments.

There were foot long ash stakes with sharp whittled points; glass bottles filled with a clear liquid; a couple of UV torches; a hand mounted crossbow with silver bolts, and various crucifixes made of silver or gold. He lifted this layer out and underneath was another foam section cut out. In this was laid a black sword pommel.

Earthborn almost lovingly picked up the pommel, his large hand wrapped around the black leather bound handle. He pressed a hidden catch, and the cross pieces of the pommel dropped down with a click. Then he triggered the hidden catch again, and this time a silver blade hissed from inside the pommel, extended about a foot and a half, and then from inside of that piece, a final, pointed piece emerged.

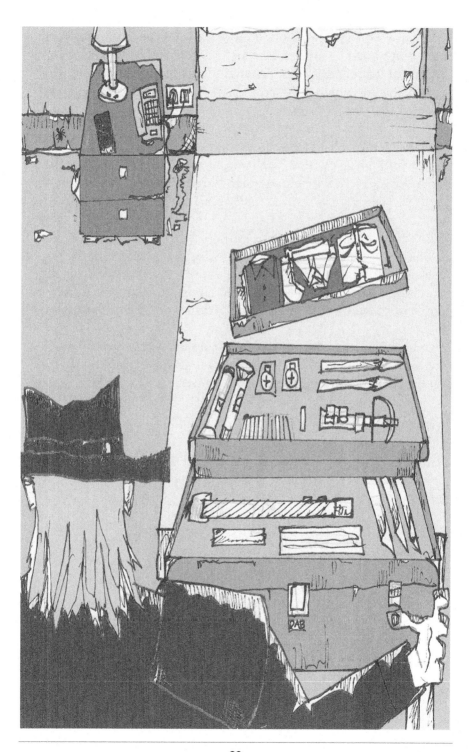

The sword was a shade under 5 foot long, and the blade was razor sharp and plated in silver. Silver did not kill THEM, but a cut from this meant it could stop them changing form for some time. It was very frustrating when you had cornered one, only for it to change into mist and dissipate away.

Similarly, the UV light from the torches would not harm them (except for a bit of eczema) but it could dazzle them and slow them down. Any advantage helped when fighting the legions of the damned. The only things that really worked were stakes and a fire.

"Hmmm, steak and a fire" thought Earthborn, and then he realized he was starving. Content that all his equipment had evaded customs (although given the unique nature of his trunk it was not surprising) he dissembled and stored all his kit away. He locked the case, scrambled the combination and turned the catches horizontal.

Then he went down to the busy bar, fully intending to murder a nice bloody steak. He was not more than 0.5 miles from his quarry, and the dirty work would start tomorrow.

Chapter Five – Kings, Queens and Bishops

"Check."

"Hmmmmm, clever young master George. You have me in a spot of difficulty, but nothing that I am not able to counter."

Sir Francis reached out a long hand, and two of his even longer fingers pinched the top of his black king, and slid it a space to the left – a white square.

"My shah is now free from your Knight Errant's challenge", he smirked.

"Ah, but you didn't notice my trap", countered George, and slid his white bishop diagonally along three white spaces.

"Check-Mate."

"Eh?" cried out Sir Francis, sounding genuinely shocked, "What have you conjured? You are as crafty as a wolf on the hunt. You have trapped me cold and dead. If I move my Shah to the right, your knight errant will run a spear through him. If I leave him where he is, then your damned pontiff has him and will ex-communicate him and send him to the dungeon and the headsman."

Sir Francis curled up his extra-long middle finger, and then flicked it out, knocking over his black king, the age old sign of acknowledging he had lost. He stood up, and bowed rather formally.

"The game is yours, sir. Well played, well played indeed. You are turning into a seasoned player of the game of Kings. And the irony has not escaped me that I was defeated by an agent of your church."

"Rematch?" asked George, eager to push his advantage and very pleased with the respect Sir Francis had accorded him. This was the first time he had defeated Sir Francis, despite numerous games. He had come close in the past, but the wily vampyr had always managed to escape his traps and win.

"No, not today, young George. I have not lost a game of chess for 500 years. I do not care to risk losing a second this day. But..."

And he leaned forward towards George, who flinched back. Varney glared at him, his eyes wide, red rimmed and hypnotic, his lips drawn back in a snarl, revealing his two long sharp fangs.

"...Know this, mortal. You may have defeated me today, but you have not vanquished me. I will have my revenge on you and all of your lineage. I will extract my vengeance in blood and pain."

And with that, he stood up and turned around dramatically, his long coat flaring out like a cape, and flounced off towards the door. Then he turned and glared at George.

George fell around laughing, and then Varney started to snigger, a strange, dry sound

"Heh heh heh, I thought I had you then, George."

"Nice try, Sir Francis", George giggled, tears of laughter rolling down his cheeks.

"Anyway, earlier on, did you not say you had been experimenting with my glood again?"

Sir Francis was keen to take the subject away from chess. Although he would never admit it, has was irked to lose to a mortal, and a child – but then again George wasn't just any mortal child.

"Ah yes, of course. I think you will like this Sir Francis. To the kitchen!" he yelled and charged out of the room. Sir Francis shook his head and said to himself,

"Ah, the enthusiasm of youth. I wish I could remember those days"

Sir Francis sighed, and followed George, except he didn't exactly charge out of the room. He more floated.

The kitchen had changed a lot. It used to be an empty shell, as it was never used. The few pieces of furniture had rotted away and collapsed in on themselves. But now it was all gleaming and new. There were new kitchen units, an oven, microwave, and various utensils and gadgets. There was also a huge double doored steel fridge.

The kitchen would be a pleasant room to spend time in, if Sir Francis hadn't insisted that everything possible should be black. In some ways Sir Francis was a bit traditional, and he didn't think it was right to install a kitchen that was plum or mint green. It was either black or blood red, and the kids didn't really fancy the latter.

In the kitchen were Flora and Henry, and also Chili and Mr. March. Chili was sitting on Floras left shoulder, surveying the room to see if there was any unguarded food he could snaffle. Mr. March was lying curled up on a rug, front paws on his nose, snoring loudly.

"Hullo, Sir Francis" piped Flora, happily. "We have been working on a problem you have."

"One of your problems", piped up Henry.

"Henry, that's not helping. But the fact that you are either blue when you are hungry, or green after you've had some glood. It does rather make you stand out."

"Sadly, too true, my girl."

"You said you wanted to go out in the world more, and we can't be here late at night. So it will have to be daytime."

"Yes! Then we can go and have adventures and not just spend all the time in this stinky house"

"Henry!" shouted George, worried that Sir Francis may be insulted, but instead he just smiled at Henry. George thought it was a smile of affection, but with Sir Francis somehow his smile made him appear more sinister.

Flora glared at Henry, who then decided it was a good idea to inspect his shoe laces with his eyes.

"So we have tried a few tweaks to the glood"

George walked over and pulled open one of the giant fridges doors. Inside were shelves and shelves of ingredients, and a couple of shelves of pre-made glood in clear glass bottles. It has a lot of shelves!

George reached in and grabbed a bottle that was a different colour to the regular glood. In fact is seemed to constantly be changing colour. He took it over to the work surface and placed it in the baby bottle heater. When the bottle was to temperature, he passed it to Sir Francis and said,

"Try this"

Sir Francis unscrewed the lid and took a swig

"Hmmmm, not bad, George, not bad at all" and then he drank the rest of the contents down in one. He put the bottle down and they all stared at him.

Slowly, his face, which had been a nice eggshell blue, changed to a mint green, but then most of the colour started to drain from his it. His teeth also started to itch, which was a weird experience to say the least.

But his face was now white, a very pale white. Paler than any human still walking had a right to be. Then he opened his mouth and felt at his teeth with his tongue. He felt them start to shrink, back into his gums. It wasn't a pleasant feeling but it wasn't exactly painful. Just odd.

"Wow", cried Henry.

"Amazing", shouted Flora.

"Hmm, that worked better than expected", mused George.

Standing before them was Sir Francis but not as they knew him. His face was still long and thin, but was pale, and his teeth had drawn back to normal human length. His ears were still pointed (and one was still bent) and his eyes were still red and glaring.

"What is in this new "glood????"

"I tried adding some ingredients that are linked to creatures who change colour. So blue, green algae – as that helps flamingos turn pink", George said

"What, really?" asked Henry, "shouldn't it be red algae"

"No, as the algae absorbs the blue and green from the sun's rays, and all you can see is red", George explained

"Oh"

"And cuttlefish ink, chameleon scales, and a few other things"

"They must have been hard to get, and quite expensive I would imagine"

"Well, I shopped around a bit" said George, quite vaguely. George hoped that Sir Francis didn't check his eBay account anytime soon as the ingredients had cost a bit. But George reasoned that firstly he was doing it for Sir Francis, and secondly it will teach Sir Francis about cyber-security, as his password was far too easy to guess (vampyrsrule, all lower case).

Fortunately Sir Francis had other things on his mind.

"How do I look?" Sir Francis asked

"Different! Your skin is very pale but with a bit of make-up..."

"Make-up?? Never!"

"Bad choice of words, George. How about the paint actor's use when they go on stage?" added Flora.

"That would be acceptable. The art of the stage is a noble one, and one that I have dabbled with, in my youth"

"Then we can put some colour in your skin so you don't look quite so..." she stopped, searching for a sensitive term

"Dead", supplied Henry

"Well, yes, dead", conceded Flora. Sir Francis looked a bit upset.

"Then a hat, that would cover your ears, and stop your head from sizzling. And a pair of sunglasses. That will hide your eyes, and maybe stop you getting too dizzy in the sunlight. We may be able to pass you off as human", continued George.

"Human?? How dare you. I am superior in every way to you paltry mortals. I am stronger than ten men, I have the knowledge of centuries, and I will..."

"Sir Francis, just so you can go out into the world with us"

"Ahh, fair enough my girl. I think I may have overreacted there"

"Hmm, maybe just a bit"

"So this is miraculous, children. To be able to walk amongst humankind again, not shunned but accepted; not feared, but welcomed; not in secret, but exposed, this would be a great thing indeed. What wonders shall we experience? What exotic places shall we see? What knowledge shall we acquire? What marvellous place should be visit first?"

"Erm, we were just thinking about the park", said Henry excitedly

"Oh"

Chapter Six – Wednesday Wonders

It was a bit late in the day to visit the park, and so they decided the next day (weather permitting) would be ideal for Sir Francis' first big day out. If walking 300 yards down the road to a field with a few swings and roundabouts a big day out.

The kids decided it would be best to be back for tea.

Henry gently prodded Mr. March with his foot, and was rewarded with one eye opening and staring at him.

"Are you coming with us Maximus?" asked Henry

They had settled into a routine with Mr. March and his two forms. When he was in human form, they still called him Mr. March. When he was in his other form, everyone called him Maximus.

"I think he better had, he has been in that shape for a few hours now. He may forget to turn back otherwise", advised George.

Maximus raised his big shaggy head, yawned with a sort of "YOWWWLLL" sound, and then licked his lips noisily. He looked at Henry and nodded. Seeing a nodding dog is quite an unusual experience and it always made Henry laugh.

"Well then, you had best go and change and get dressed!", suggested Flora.

Part of the problem with changing into his other form was that when he changed back to human, he was always naked. Although his tall, rangy body was so naturally hairy, he still looked like he was half wolf and half clothed. Initially, when they had gone out with him in his canine, or is it lupine, form they had never thought to take a set of clothes. It was quite embarrassing when he needed to turn back, and they had to resort to "borrowing" a blanket from someone's washing line.

Maximus stalked off, his long claws click-clacking against the tiled floor. He slipped off into the downstairs loo, and started the process to change.

There was a lot of grunting, groaning and moaning. The process is not quick and not painless. A few minutes later, Mr. March staggered through the door. He was a bit untidy, and trying to straighten his tie. Sweat drenched his brow, and he was breathing deeply.

"WOWLLLL......sorry......frog in my throat."

"Sure it's not a dog?" asked Henry, grinning.

Mr. March smiled down on Henry and reached out and ruffled his hair. It seemed only fair, as Henry spent a lot of time rearranging his hair when he was Maximus.

"Well, we had better get going", Mr. March said "We don't want Mrs. Bannerworth upset at us, do we?"

In fact, Mrs. Bannerworth was very rarely upset at them – despite the time that they spent at the strange house. They four of them, sorry, five as Chili was still perched on Flora's shoulder, crossed the road towards number 99.

The door was on the latch and so they all walked in. Mrs. Bannerworth was standing at the hob, tapping her feet to the radio. She was making what she called her Wednesday Wonder – which more often than not was far from wonderful. It wasn't a specific dish, it was more what was left in the fridge before the food delivery was due on Thursday. Tonight smelt like left over chilli (the meal!) mixed with cabbage, spinach and sweetcorn.

"Ah the fabulous five have returned from the house of hell for the day" she said, as she reached for her tall clear glass of straw coloured bubbles and had a sip. "How is our vampyric overlord today?"

The kids were still unsure how much she believed about Sir Francis. She seemed quite relaxed about the fact they spent a lot of time in an old house, with a man she had never met (and never seemed to have the inclination to meet), who said he was a vampyr. It was partly as Mr. March was with them, and she trusted him; but mainly that she trusted the children and their judgement.

"We made new glood for him mama", shouted Henry excitedly.

"Yes, this one turns him pale and shrinks his teeth, mummy", continued Flora.

"Mother, the plan is to try to take him out to the park tomorrow, so he's not just stuck in that old house", completed George.

"But he does look at pale as a ghost, mama."

"Can I borrow some blusher, mummy?" asked Flora. She had not yet been allowed to buy her own make up, but often borrowed her mum's. Or, to be honest, nicked it.

"Yes of course, sweetie. You know where it is."

Flora bounded to the stairs, Chili still glued to her shoulder. She popped into her mum's room and found the blusher and put it in her jacket pocket. Just in case, she also borrowed a lipstick (although whether this was for Sir Francis is debatable). They rushed back down to the kitchen, just in time for food.

"Oh, whilst it's on my mind, Flora, you didn't borrow my silver bracelet for dressing up, did you?"

"No, mummy."

"Oh, OK. I must have misplaced it. Never mind. Anyway everyone – tuck in. Except for you, mister", Mrs. Bannerworth said, pointing at Chili.

Dinner was not an unmitigated disaster, it was more a slight misadventure. Still it was hot food after a busy day, and so they managed to just about clean their plates. Mr. March positively and almost literally wolfed it down, and was staring hopefully at the bowl in case there were seconds.

"Anyway, you three. Who is it that needs baths or showers tonight? Sort yourselves out. If you are having a big day out tomorrow you need a good night's sleep."

"But what about Chili? He needs to go back to Sir Francis' house."

"Well, I suppose if he's good, then he can stay here tonight. But if that creature raids my fridge again, then tomorrow night's tea will be Chili chilli."

Flora was pretty sure she was joking. Chili was not so, and tried to stare innocently at the ceiling.

The three children grumbled a bit but trudged upstairs and started to fight about who was going in the shower last, and therefore would get only cold water. George lost.

Downstairs, Mrs. Bannerworth looked at Mr. March, who had left the table and was slouching on the sofa. "Erm, Mr. Marchingdale, you know the rules. I cook, you clean."

Mr. March grumbled but managed to lever himself back up. He started to stack all the dinner plates.

Chapter Seven – A Grand Day Out (Almost)

"Do you think that will do?" asked Flora.

"Maybe a bit more on the left cheek?" suggested Henry.

Flora dabbed away, and then stood back and looked at Sir Francis quizzically. He had tried another cup of the new glood, and once again he was as pale as a wraith. Flora had applied the blusher with about as much skill as you would expect from an 8 year old. It was smeared all over his face to try to give him rosy cheeks. He looked a bit like a mannequin, but at least he didn't look undead (or dead).

"It's good enough" pronounced George, "we don't know how much time we have. Sir Francis, after we left, how long was it before you turned back to, erm…."

"Abnormal?" suggested Henry.

"As close to normal as you are." carried on George, just glancing in mild annoyance at Henry.

"I am afraid I do not really know, young George."

"But you could have timed it?"

"Well, one of the things about being long lived is that you don't tent to…"

"Pay much attention to time", the three kids finished in unison.

"Oh, it would appear I have said this before."

"Just a few times, Sir Francis", said Flora, kindly.

"Well, I would say it was definitely after the Repair Shop started, but before Love Island finished. Aside from that, then I really do not know."

"If you don't know the time, then how do you know what time to watch TV?"

"I set reminders of course!" said Sir Francis proudly. Part of the change in Sir Francis' life (or un-life) was that since electricity and Wi-Fi had been installed, and then smart TV's and laptops soon followed. A whole world of soap operas, reality TV and documentaries (which is what Sir Francis called vampyr films) had opened up for him.

"So, maybe 4-5 hours?" estimated George, setting an alarm on his phone. "In which case we had better get going."

They looked at Sir Francis. He was wearing a pair of jeans, trainers, and a plain black jacket that didn't look like a cape. On his head, he had a baseball cap, under which his long ears had been strapped to his head with bandages. His look was completed by a pair of wraparound shades.

"So, the sunglasses should help with the dizziness, the hat with the eczema. Anything else?"

"No I do not think so, my boy. Let us make haste to this paradise you call "The Park". I am intrigued to experience its splendor."

"Might be expecting a bit much", Henry whispered to Maximus, who was as usual by his side. Maximus laughed, which in this case meant flopping his long tongue out and panting a couple of times.

It wasn't a long walk to the park, but as they went, they were excited by the day out. They walked down the street in full sunlight. The sun hammered down on Sir Francis, but he felt surprisingly OK. He stuck his arm out into the sun, and saw a little bit of hissing as it singed some small hairs from the back of his hand.

George led the way, with Sir Francis at his side. As they went, George pointed out things of interest to Varney. The sparrows in the

hedgerows. Bees buzzing amongst the flowers, and the toy shop that George really wanted to get a Star Wars Lego set from.

Behind them came Flora, with Chili for once not on her shoulder. Instead, due to his colouring, they decided he would be better in Flora's backpack. After them came Henry and Maximus, who constantly ran circles around the group. Everything seemed perfect.

However, if they had paid attention (and you would think they would after what happened to them last time), they would have noticed they were being followed. A battered old VW camper van was following them, creeping along the kerb, keen to not lose sight of them. It spluttered along, its exhaust belching out thick smoke as it shuddered on.

At the wheel, staring incessantly at the tall gangly figure of Varney, was an average man with red hair and rectangular spectacles with coloured lenses. On the dashboard was a video camera, filming. On the small 4 inch screen, there was an image of the kids, Maximus and Varney – or rather there was of an image of the kids and Maximus. All there was of Sir Francis was a floating baseball cap and pair of shades.

The driver spoke into a digital voice recorder as he drove.

"10:21 am on Thursday 29th July, in transit to unknown location. Target is in sight, with 3 children believed to be the Bannerworth children, 99 Shackledown Avenue; and a large dog, breed undetermined. I have an eyeball on them all, including the subject.

But the subject does not show on digital video equipment. I suspect some sort of cloaking device. Maybe the type used in Roswell in 1947. Or a reality field. Or possibly some other extraterrestrial technology I have yet to encounter. But this is a real life situation. I am in contact with the subject and will continue my surveillance."

Tuesday clicked off the recording device for now, and continued to follow at a snail's pace.

Eventually the group reached the park, and Tuesday pulled his van onto the kerb and turned the engine off. It shuddered to a halt.

Tuesday slipped out of the van. Or rather he tried to open the door and found it was stuck, again. He cursed under his breath as he realized he had forgotten to bring a can of WD40. He hammered and kicked away at the door until it eventually gave way. Unfortunately it gave way just before Tuesday threw his shoulder at the door and as it had now swung open, Tuesday's shoulder came into contact with only thin air – or slightly less than thin air due to the noxious fumes that enveloped the van from its own exhaust.

He tumbled to the ground, and did a paratrooper's roll to get straight to his feet. At least he did in his mind, but all he ended up doing was lying on his back with his feet over his head in a very undignified way. He lay there, like a riggwelter, unable to get off his back for a few moments. Eventually he rocked enough to roll over to one side and he managed to scramble to his feet. He looked around, red faced, and saw that no one was paying any attention to him.

He grabbed his binoculars and his Pentax ME Super and hung them around his neck, and headed for the trees overlooking the park.

In the park below, the kids were enjoying themselves immensely. Flora was busy trying to go all the way over on the swings, and then hanging precariously upside down by her knees on the jungle gym. Chili, meanwhile, allowed out of the backpack, scampered up and down all the rope bridges and fireman's poles.

("Click, click, click" went the camera on the hill)

Meanwhile, Henry was on a roundabout (no! not that type), and he had tied Maximus' lead to one of the handles and shouted at Maximus to run faster and faster. The great wolf complied, and ran around in circles, dragging the roundabout went faster and faster. Henry shouted in joy, until he started to feel a bit green himself, and yelped for Maximus to stop. His lupine friend did just that, suddenly, and then found himself being dragged around for a moment for the momentum of the heavy ride. Eventually they stopped, Maximus as a heap on the floor, and Henry on top of him. They lie there exhausted, and a bit battered, and then they got up and did the whole thing again.

George and Sir Francis were on the see-saw. Despite their (considerable) age difference, and that Sir Francis was nearly a foot taller, they were actually about the same weight and so a good balance for the ride. They bounced up and down merrily, and Sir Francis found a strange noise starting to emanate from his throat,

"Heh heh heh heh", and he realized in shock that he was laughing, with joy. Normally most vampyrs only laugh at others misfortunes, like when poor Vernon fell on a fence post and accidentally staked himself.

However, this newfound joy meant he got carried away. As they bounced, Varney pushed with his feet harder and harder. Given that he was far stronger than a human, when he was at the top of his upward arc, he threw himself downwards, and landed with great force. Poor George on the other end flew up really fast and was thrown up into the air. He squealed as he started to fly (or plummet) through the air. Sir Francis's grimace like smile turned into a grimace like grimace as he realized what he had done.

With preternatural speed, he leapt from his seat and ran over to where George was now heading towards the ground, and caught him as easily as a man would catch a rabbit (although why a man would want to play catch with a rabbit is another story).

("Click click click" went the camera on the hill).

Sir Francis put George back on terra firma, although it wasn't that firm as the floor of the play park was covered in 6 inch deep bark.

"George, my boy, I must apologize most profusely. One forgets one's own strength sometimes."

"It's OK, Sir Francis, it was quite good fun actually. It was almost like flying until the last bit where I was falling."

The kids made the most of the play park, each having to try each piece of equipment at least three times. The zip-wire proved particularly popular, and Maximus' tail wagged continually as he pulled the occupants along and then let them go. Then he chased after them, his tongue hanging out in a wolf's smile.

It was now past noon, and they were all hungry. They sat under a shaded tree, and rummaged in their bags and found their sandwiches and crisps. They sat down and munched away, ravenous. Henry, when he thought no one was looking, kept throwing Wotsits and carrot sticks to Maximus, who of course didn't say no. No one had thought to bring a drink for Sir Francis, who just sat there patiently waiting. One major advantage of being so old is that you do tend to learn how to be patient, as sometimes decades pass by without anything happening.

("Click click clack clack" went the camera on the hill. The film needed changing).

They finished their lunches, and put any rubbish in the already overflowing bin, trying to avoid the suspicious black bags with bunny rabbit ears.

"How about we go down to the pond?" asked Flora.

Henry and George both nodded in agreement and they all set off.

"Sir Francis?"
"Yes, my dear boy."

"You are floating again."

"Oops, my apologies."

Chapter Eight – Watching the Detective

Up on the hill, Tuesday was frantically was trying to change the film in the camera when the group headed towards the pond. Despite the world's inexorable march towards digital photography, Tuesday had stubbornly stayed in the bygone era of 35mm films. In the bright sunshine, it was hard to change the film without exposing it to the rays of light –which would ruin the photos.

His Pentax ME Super was one of his prize possessions and went everywhere with him. It's something that children today might find incomprehensible, in the back of it was a roll of film that created a photo when exposed to light – pretty much the same way that photographs were taken in the 19th century.

But Tuesday persisted with 35mm black and white film for two main reasons. First of all, he did not trust digital photographs. They could be altered, photoshopped, filtered far too easily - whereas the negative from a film camera you can trust. Secondly, he enjoyed developing the films in his dark room (which was in fact the bathroom in his small flat). Dark rooms are a bit of a misnomer really, as they are more red rooms. There was a third reason really, in that he was just very stuck in his ways and didn't like a lot of change.

He managed to change the film, and stow away the used one for developing later, and then he ran down the hill to catch up with his quarry. Ran is probably the wrong word to use here, he more trotted and stumbled. He disliked physical exercise with a passion that bordered on religious.

Fortunately he was only a few minutes behind Varney and the kids, and he caught up with them as they stood at the edge of the pond. Ducks of various shapes and sizes and makes and models quacked incessantly. Geese honked and fluttered their huge wings rather aggressively. Swans floated by serenely.

Henry and Flora had kept the crusts from their sandwiches, and were getting great delight from chucking pieces into the pond and watching the various birds race for each treat. George knew that bread wasn't the best food for ducks, but decided to stay quiet as he reasoned a couple of crusts wouldn't harm them. Maximus kept trying to dart into the water, chasing the ducks, but would then quickly turn around when confronted by a goose. Not even a werewolf really wants to fight an enraged goose. Their wings can break a man's arm, don't you know?

("Click click click" went the camera, this time from a bush about 100 yards from the kids. If anyone was anywhere near the bush, they might have been slightly perturbed to hear deep breathing and panting coming from behind the leaves and branches. Tuesday was still knackered from running downhill).

Sir Francis was leaning against a railing, enjoying the simple things in life (or un-life). He smiled as Maximus was chased almost the full length of the pond by a gaggle of enraged geese, their wings flared up like a horde of extremely annoyed angels. But as he smiled, he felt a pin prick against his lips. He stopped, dead still. He opened his mouth and slowly ran a long finger against his top gum. Nothing, but then a bump, and the feel of a fang poking through the gums. Then the fang started to grow until it was an inch long.

Then he felt his skin, which was tingling and warm. Strange as he normally had a steady body temperature of about 5 degrees. He yelped and tapped George on his shoulder. George turned around and looked at the perturbed vampyr.

"Oh dear, that doesn't look good."

Sir Francis shook his head, agitatedly.

"Do you think the glood is wearing off?"

Sir Francis nodded, frantically.

"Flora, Henry, CODE BLUE", George started. The other two stopped dead as they had been well drilled in this contingency plans. George liked contingency plans. Flora, not so much.

Henry, rather appropriately, wolf whistled for the wolf, who turned his head and raced back from the other side of the pond, scattering the geese who could now see that Maximus was not playing. Henry attached the lead back onto Maximus' collar. They didn't like using a lead and collar but it was decided it was best when he was out in public, Maximus should look like a domestic dog (except he didn't really).

"We need to get home now, or back to Ratpole ideally", said George.

"I fear it is too late, dear boy", said Sir Francis.

His face was blotchy and spotted with blue blobs of colour. One of his fangs had grown back to its full length. The second fang was trying to grow back in a sort of Harryhausen style animation. Sir Francis panicked a bit, and held his head in his long hands, knocking off his cap and shades. His face was now once again long and blue, with eyes shrouded in deep sockets, and his two fangs protruding from under his top lip. The bandages came loose, and his long pointed ears popped into view.

Behind the bush, Tuesday stopped in amazement, his camera held limply in his hands. It was true! All of it! All of articles in the Fortean Times he had read, all the blurred photos he had seen on-line. All of the conspiracy theories he had read about the US government and Area 51. But they weren't little green men. They were tall, blue men, with poor dental hygiene, and they were walking amongst us. Here, in Bedlamton of all places.

Regaining his composure he raised his camera.

"Click click click, click click click."

Chapter Nine – Crows and Old Straw

There was a sizzling sound, as the bright sun started to flake the bald head of Sir Francis, and he staggered as a dizzy spell overcame him. Maximus dashed in, and caught the ailing vampyr on his broad, furry back.

The children knew that the sun wouldn't cause Sir Francis any real damage, but they were more concerned about people noticing the bald, stick thin blue man with pointy teeth and ears.

"Henry, get Maximus' coat from my backpack."

"Roger that", said Henry.

"Roger who?" asked Sir Francis, clearly confused.

Henry grabbed George's backpack and unzipped it. He pulled out Maximus', or rather Mr. March's, tweed jacket. They had learnt the hard way not to go out without a change of clothes for the wolf, in case he had to change his skin. This was after that rather embarrassing incident in the window of the ice cream parlour on Trundle Street.

Henry passed the jacket to George, who threw it over Sir Francis' head to cover it and hide his face. The hat and shades were clearly ineffectual now. Then they huddled around the vampyr to provide him some protection, although the fact that he was a good 2 feet taller than George made this a rather limited tactic.

They left the park, walking as fast as they could, but not too fast to draw too much attention. A woman with her young child noticed them and started to stare, so George nudged Henry, who whistled. With that, at the pre-arranged signal, the great wolf started to run around in circles, trying to catch his own tail, whilst barking incessantly. The child prodded her mother, as he stared and laughed at the silly dog. The woman looked down at her happy child and started to laugh, and forgot about the strange man.

They hurried back, taking a more direct route as George didn't need to go past the toy shop again. They didn't notice the camper van slowly following them.

They were at the edge of town, where it started to change into farmland. They walked along the lane, with fields to their right. Then they heard a laugh from over the fence.

"Heh heh heh, looks like you are in a spot of bother, Master Bannerworth. It serves you well, for the inconvenience you caused me", laughed a familiar voice.

Despite their hurry, they all stopped and walked to the fence. On the other side, in the middle of a field, was a familiar figure. He was short, except also tall, with straw-like hair pasted over his forehead. His thin face sneered down at them.

"Well, well, look who it is. It's that's rotten sack of brushwood. But he seems to be in rather reduced circumstances", laughed George.

Mr. Sticks hissed in annoyance, and replied,

"Just a temporary inconvenience, Master Bannerworth. I cut ties with Miss Words and had to find alternative employment, but this is just temporary."

"Sacked more like" chuckled Flora.

"Yes he looks like a sack of…"

"Henry!" George cried.

"Sorry."

Mr. Sticks glared down at them from up on his perch, as he seemed to have found a temporary job. He was suspended on top of a long pole, that was stuck in the ground, with his arms tied to a cross piece. His old suit was ragged and torn, and hits of hay and twigs poked through the holes. He was wearing a battered straw hat and had a red neckerchief around his scrawny throat.

"He's a scarecrow", cried Henry, laughing.

"Well, after you rather disarmed myself and my associate, I did not have exactly the choice of vocations. But know this, Bannerworths, and your miserable mutt. I will rise again. I will be back to get my revenge. I will be- Owwwwww!"

His monologue was ruined when a large black crow swooped down and pecked out one of his eyes, and flew off squawking (or more accurately, crowing) happily.

"Oh not again, it will take me days to grow a new one", lamented Sticks.

"Well, looks like he is about as good a scarecrow as he was an evil henchman", laughed George, and the other two fell about laughing. They even heard a few dry coughs from Sir Francis that served as his laugh.

"Gloat whilst you can, Master Bannerworth, as you have not heard the last of, oh get away you imbecilic feathered vermin", he cried as another crow (or the same one) landed on his shoulder, and started to help himself to pieces of Sticks, presumably to use in its nest.

"Oh, the ignominy", Sticks muttered, resigned to his fate.

"And anyway, you signed a contract saying that you couldn't hurt us – and that's legally, and mystically, binding", George reminded Sticks.

"Pish posh, contracts. Any goblin, ghoul or wraith knows that there is always wriggle room in any contract, so we will be ....Ow, stop it you foul flying rat" as the crow returned for another nibble, causing more laughter amongst the Bannerworth party.

"We had best get back to Ratpole House, and leave this poor fellow to his fate", suggested George, wiping tears from his eyes (the kind of joy, not sadness).

"Not yet", replied Flora and she turned back to Sticks "So where's your friend? The one I eroded down to a head?" she demanded of Sticks, who had somehow managed to fight off the crow.

"Hrmpuh, he is still in the same sorry situation you put him in, but he has also found gainful employment."

"Doing what?" queried Henry.

"He's an ornamental statue in the garden of a local stately home", admitted Sticks, glumly.

Once again they all laughed and then turned their backs on Sticks, and walked off.

From behind them they heard Sticks continue to rage "Just you wait, Bannerworths, and your craven cur, I will return to wreak my revenge and to.......Oww, not you again, stop it you filthy carrion eater."

They carried on past the field and soon were back at the relative haven of Ratpole House.

"Click click click", went the camera not far away.

Chapter Ten – Sticky Carpets and Dark Rooms

When the kids, along with their various paranormal pals, were back inside Ratpole House, Tuesday finally put down his camera, and placed the lens cap on it. He had 6 rolls of 35mm film to develop and he was sure he had some great shots of the alien revealing his true self. He had seen it often enough on TV that aliens were able to change forms to look human – but finally he had proof.

He turned the van's engine on, and black smoke belched out of the exhaust and it shuddered to life. He drove off to the other side of town, back to his flat. Little did he realise that the watcher was being watched. Over the other side of the road, a tall figure in a long coat and wide brimmed hat leaned laconically against a lamppost, watching.

From his pocket he took a small device that looked like a cross between a smartphone and a radio. He flicked a switch and the screen flickered to life, showing a map of Bedlamton, and a flashing red dot. The dot was moving at about 20 miles an hour to the other side of town. The figure grunted in satisfaction. He lowered his hat brim even further down and started to stalk off in the direction of the blinking red dot, taking long strides. His boots clicked against the pavement, and his coat swished dramatically behind him.

Oblivious to the fact he had become the prey, Tuesday arrived back home to his BOP (base of operations – which was in fact just a small second floor flat in a Victorian townhouse). He jumped out of the van, or more fell out in stages, and grabbed hold of all his equipment. He searched for his key, finally finding it in the last pocket he looked in. Keys tend to do that. He cursed in impatience until he found it, and slipped it in the lock on the third attempt – as his hands were trembling so much with excitement and irritation.

He stepped inside and flicked the light switch. Overhead the single bulb flickered and stuttered, and then eventually decided to do its job and come on properly.

The flat was a masterpiece in drab. All the furniture was tired and drab, light browns, off white creams, off cream whites. The drab curtains were puce, and the net curtains behind them were yellowed with age. The drab carpet was the type you would find in a pub in the 1970's, and in about as good a condition. Tuesday's shoes seem to stick to it as he tried to walk across it, and he could feel his hair start to stick up on end from the buildup of static from the cheap nylon blend.

He went straight to his dark room, and yelped as he got an electric shock when he touched the metal door handle. The door pushed open into a bathroom, which had been converted into a dark room, if converting a room just involved dumping a lot of stuff that shouldn't be there in it.

He turned on the red bulb overhead, and got to work. He had several trays, with various liquids, and he got the reels of film out and processed them, and waited for them to develop. When it was safe, he left the room and pulled his video camera out of the bag. He watched in amazement and disappointment as the footage showed the activities of the kids, the large ugly dog, and the strange green ferret – but no images of his prime target, Alien X (as he had decided to call it, partly as he used up the names Aliens A to T on hoaxes, and then decided to jump from T to X as it sounded cooler than Alien U).

However, what could be seen were the cap and the sunglasses floating down the street.

"So", reasoned Tuesday to himself "Maybe X has a cloaking field but it is limited, and does not cover items of this earth?"

That the baseball cap was from earth was pretty clear from the fact it had the crest of Bedlamton United, the local football team, on its front. It seemed unlikely that United merchandise had spread to outlets in the outer spiral arm of the galaxy. It was hard enough to get a replica shirt even in town.

Frustrated, but aware that he still had good footage that showed I.F.A activity (Identified Flying Accessories), he stopped the tape and removed it, and labelled it and put it on a shelf with countless others.

He returned to the dark room, and the prints were ready. He pegged them onto a clothes line that was spread about head height in front of the bath. Then he waited. Slowly images came together of the kids, then the dog, and then the ferret creature. But nothing of Alien X. Bitter disappointment filled his mouth, and he turned and punched the wall in frustration. The punch did little or no damage to the wall, but caused Tuesday to yelp in pain.

What to do now. He had nothing – except floating glasses and hats. That was hardly enough for the mainstream press. He placed his hands on the sink, and then leaned down, crushing disillusionment filling him. Then he got up, and turned back round and stopped still, shocked.

Something odd was happening to the photos. He had always tried to get pictures of Alien X in the centre of each photos, and now the gaps where he should have been were changing. Slowly on each picture a ghostly picture of Alien X appeared. Each was slightly out of focus. Then, even more remarkably, for photos of Sir Francis' transformation back into his usual self he turned blue on the prints.

That was impossible. This was a black and white film, and should only develop black and white images. But here they were. Close up pictures of Varney, no hat or glasses, blue skinned with pointed ears and teeth. Tuesday yelped in pleasure and, checking they were dry, unpegged the photos and went back into the living room (which is quite an inappropriate term for a room no one would really want to live in).

He went to the fridge in the small galley kitchenette, and took out an iced tea and sat down in the old armchair. He beamed in

excitement as he looked through each picture again and again. He cracked open the seal on the bottle of the iced tea and took a long swig in celebration. Tuesday really knew how to celebrate. Then he leaned back and relaxed, closing his eyes.

All was quiet in the flat, but then from outside he heard footsteps. Loud footsteps, made by a heavy tread on the bare floorboards of the landing. The footsteps were getting louder, and seemed to be approaching his flat. They had the steady even tread of a person who was determined to get somewhere. Someone that sounded implacable, unstoppable. Tuesday got all of this just from the footsteps.

Then they stopped, right outside his door. He peered down and saw the dim light from the landing under the gap in the door. But now, two shadows were interrupting this light. Then the door handled turned. The door was locked (Tuesday was a stickler for security, as he never knew when the government would turn up to seize his research).

He sensed frustration from the being behind the door. Then there was a knock on the door, although a knock doesn't really capture it. When you knock on a friend's door, it's normally a light rat-a-tat-tat. This was a booming thud. Then another. Then another. The door shook in its frame. Tuesday panicked and hid behind the chair, unsure of what to do. He peeped around, his eyes locked on the door.

The booming knock stopped, and all was quiet for a few moments that felt like weeks. Then there was a massive crash, and the splintering of wood. The door flew open, almost flying off its hinges with the force. The Yale locks were simply wrenched from the door and door frame. A huge boot was in the centre of the doorway, which slowly found its proper place back on the floorboards.

A huge figure filled what was left of the door frame. Filled to overflowing, as Tuesday could only see the legs, torso and chin of the man. The rest of his face was too high up for the space. The figure ducked down and entered the room and looked around.

Tuesday ducked back behind the chair, but too late. The narrow eyes saw their quarry, and the figure stalked across the room, and with a casual swipe of its long arm, pushed the heavy chair out of the way. The chair flew halfway across the room and landed with a thud.

Tuesday looked up at the terrifying figure, and giggled nervously.

Then the figure spoke for the first time.

"I don't think it's nice you laughing", he whispered, and then leaned down towards Tuesday, a large hand reaching for him.

Chapter Eleven – Changes

"How are you feeling, Sir Francis?" enquired Flora, politely. When they had got back, they had given Sir Francis some traditional green glood, and put some after sun on his frazzled scalp. Sir Francis noted the glood tasted a bit different to usual but still drank it back in one go.

"Much improved, thank you, dear girl. It is nice to be back in the dark. I was born to the dark......"

"Oh stop it, Sir Francis, I know you are just quoting that Batman film you watched the other night", George chirped in. Sir Francis hadn't even really enjoyed the film, as the batman didn't really live up to his expectations. Varney had expected him to be part bat.

Sir Francis looked a bit crestfallen, which turned to irritation, which soon blossomed into full blown anger. *"Sometimes George was just a bit too clever for his own good. For his insolence I should rip his head from his.........."* He thought.

Sir Francis stopped. Where did that come from? He hadn't felt like exsanguinating a human for months. He shook his head in surprise and pushed the dark thought to the back of his mind. But it didn't completely disappear, and still lurked there.

Mr. March strolled in. "That was a bit odd", he said, trying to dry his thick bushy hair, which wasn't having any of it and just sprang back up in spikes.

"What. Mr. M?" asked Henry.

"It took me much longer to change back than usual. It's almost like I couldn't, or didn't want to."

"You must have been spending too much time in your other form, Mr. March" suggested Flora.

"You don't want to become like Chili do you?" George mentioned.

"By fang and claw, no. I like both my forms, and want to keep both of them."

"Then maybe a few days of staying in your two legged form?" suggested Flora.

"Good idea. Righto. No changing for me for a week."

Henry looked distinctly glum at the thought of not having a wolf to play with for a whole seven days. Mr. March noticed him looking sad and said,

"Cheer up Henry, we will still have loads of fun."

Henry smiled weakly. "I suppose. By the way, you still have your collar on."

"By jingo, so I do, thank you Henry."

Flora was busy searching in her back-pack.

"Hmm, that's odd", she said.

"What is?" replied George.

"I am sure that I put my Alice band in here, but I can't seem to find it. And it's my favourite."

"Maybe Steeple stole it?", suggested Henry.

"I doubt it, Steeple tends to haunt the second floor of Ratpole and we haven't been up there for ages", replied Flora.

"It'll be somewhere at home, somewhere undiscovered in your room. Probably between the Ark of the Covenant and the Holy Grail', laughed George. Flora's room was famously messy, and things could easily get lost in there for weeks, months or forever.

Flora thought about replying, and decided that George didn't deserve the attention. And so she just stuck her tongue out at him.

"Well, that was an exciting day. Maybe we should go home now for some tea." Mr. March said.

"I suppose so", agreed Flora, somewhat reluctantly, but she was feeling quite peckish. Even hungry enough to tackle mum's cooking.

Henry was born hungry and so took little persuading. Henry liked food, along with diggers and tractors.

They filed out, and started the short walk to number 99.

It had been an exciting, incident filled day, and surely tomorrow would be a lot quieter. Or so they thought.

Chapter Twelve – Beer and Brandy

Earthborn cleaned up the debris and any evidence and left the grotty flat. He was pleased with his progress, as pleased as he ever was with anything. The mortal Tuesday suspected nothing about Varney's true nature. The fool thought he was some sort of alien. Earthborn almost laughed at the absurdity. Almost. Always humans were looking to the stars for other life, and yet failed to see those that lived amongst them.

Fortunately no one had informed any human authorities about the disturbance on floor two. Earthborn had no fear in confronting earthly agents such as the police, but he preferred subterfuge over violence. At least at this stage.

He checked his mission log. He had his usual three point plan. To just eliminate the target was too easy, too dull, and too pedestrian. He could have done that this very day and been back on a flight to Eastern Europe, the Russian Steppes, or wherever he was needed next. But he didn't like to work that way.

The mission was progressing well, as expected. All his missions progressed well, as he was meticulous in his planning and always had a contingency plan. Or several.

The log read:

Stage 1: Segregation, status: in progress. Initial seeds have been sown. It will take time for them to grow and bloom.

Stage 2: Disclosure, status: initiated. By using another mortal agent, this has started and is expected to advance quickly.

Stage 3: Obliteration, status: in planning stage.

He would spend the next couple of days watching to see if the fruits of his endeavors were ripening. He reflected on his days labour and decided all was in place for now. As he walked back to his hotel room, he noticed a pub. He decided he had earnt a few pints of human ale – despite it being relatively bland to his taste – and maybe even a brandy or two. At least that had a bit more fire. And some food. And if the pub was lively, maybe a quick fight. He always felt a bit tetchy when his plans were in motion – and a good punch up would help alleviate that tension. Nothing too serious to alert the police.

He strode into the pub, and the room went quiet. If there had been someone there playing a piano, they no doubt would also have stopped. But obviously Michael Bubble wasn't playing tonight. All the locals stared at him. In a room of jeans and tracksuits, baseball caps and trainers, he did look a bit out of place. Or more accurately a lot out of place. He looked like a gunfighter from a long-gone era.

He strode to the bar. The crowd parted in front of him. He said,

"Ale, a pint, and brandy, and leave the bottle."

The surprised landlady replied "I'm sorry love, we don't sell brandy by the bottle. The law says it has to be in 35ml or multiples thereof."

"Fine", Earthborn grunted. "A pint of ale, and 21 shots of brandy"

The landlady, Mary, looked a bit flabbergasted, but then Earthborn pulled out a drawstring purse, and emptied a couple of gold coins onto the puddle stained bar.

Mary's eyes lit up as she recognized them as doubloons (she loved her daytime TV antique shows, and had once been on Bargain Hunt. She scooped up the coins and bit them. This is what everyone did when given gold coins and so she felt she had to. They tasted like, well, metal. But satisfied from the weight, and her knowledge of the Elizabeth Duke range at Argos, she was convinced they were gold. She stowed them away – but not in the till. She pulled the ale and started on pouring the brandies.

The pint lasted less than a few seconds, downed in one, as Earthborn drank it as parched ground absorbs water. Then two brandies and another pint. He stood at the bar, waiting. He didn't have to wait too long.

"Well, what do we have here?" asked a male voice from beside him.
"Looks like he's walked in from the Rio Grande", joked another
"Got lost on his way to Westworld"
"Thinks he's John Wayne"
"Or that guy from the spaghetti westerns"
"Maybe he's the Magnificent One"
They all laughed.

Earthborn turned around and leant on the bar, which made the bar groan a bit under his weight. He surveyed the group of lads. All were in their early twenties, wearing a mis-match of tracksuits and denim. They all had short hair, with razor sharp side partings, gelled back. The tallest was almost a match for Earthborn in height. Almost.

"I don't think it's nice, you laughing", Earthborn muttered, in a voice as quiet as the grave.
Then he turned back to the landlady, saying,

"Get three ambulances ready"

As he turned back, the tallest of the lads launched a punch at him. It hit him square on the jaw, but Earthborn didn't even move. Instead he just smiled, and cracked his knuckles, and balled his fingers into fists. Chaos ensued.

Chapter Thirteen – The Rage

After such a busy day in the park, they all decided that spending a day at Ratpole House would be a better idea. When it says they all decided, in reality George did. It was a shame as there was a comic convention in town, and they were hoping to go to it – in cos-play of course. Sir Francis, with a bit of make-up, would have made a fantastic Master from 'Salem's Lot.[1]

Henry was still moping a bit, as he didn't have a wolf to play with. Flora was still pre-occupied, as now she couldn't find her favourite necklace. Only George seemed as happy as normal, as he quite liked time inside.

They arrived at Ratpole House early afternoon. Sir Francis tended to sleep until late morning, but was normally up in time for "Loose Women". When they arrived he was in the kitchen, head inside the large fridge, grabbing himself a cup of glood. He put it in the baby bottle warmer and then drank it down.

"Ah there you are children. I must apologise for causing such a kerfuffle yesterday."

"It's not your fault, Sir Francis, it's just knowing what the limits of the new glood are."

"Yes I have stuck to the original flavour today", said Sir Francis, "Speaking of which, have you tweaked the recipe? It seems to be a bit different. It has a bit more, how shall I put this, body to it."

"No, it's all the same. Maybe it's just slightly different quantities of ingredients."

---

[1] A seriously scary vampyr!

"Yes, that must be it, Flora", agreed the vampyr. "Fancy a game of chess, George my boy?"

"Indeed! I am determined to beat you again."

"And you may well do. Your skill and knowledge is progressing alarmingly fast."

The two of them wandered off into the parlour to play.

Flora was still upset, but Chili did his best to cheer her up and eventually they went upstairs to play hide and seek. That left Henry and Mr. March, who was also in a quiet mood, but more pensive than sulking, as Henry was.

They sat there in silence for a few minutes, until Mr. March broke under pressure.

"C'mon, Henry, I know you like me in my furry shape best, but we can still have fun when I am on two legs. How about we go outside and make a den, or climb some trees?"

"I suppose", said Henry, looking a bit brighter. They both headed towards the door.

"Something has been bothering me though, Henry."

"What's that?"

"Well, every time I try to change back to human, it's getting harder and harder. I really am a bit worried that one day I will get stuck."

"Then maybe Flora's right. A few days as a human will help."

"Here's hoping, my boy, here's hoping", said Mr. March, still not convinced.

Back in the parlour, George and Sir Francis were hunched over a black and white checkered board. Sir Francis, as usual, had insisted on being black, but they always took it in turns as to who went first. The game was progressing. Sir Francis had opened with the Charlemagne gambit, but George countered with Sigurd. This lead to Sir Francis employing Achilles. But George was expecting this, and used Perseus to take the black queen.

"Blast and damn it" cursed Sir Francis, who knew his back was against the wall, both figuratively, and literally as he was sat in front of the parlour wall. Losing his queen had given George a significant advantage, and George did not give his advantage up. Soon he had Sir Francis in check, using the Kojiro Endgame to devastating effect. Sir Francis realized he would be in check mate in no more than three moves, and placed his long finger on his shah, and flicked him over.

"You triumph, my boy, a most masterfully played game. The day is yours", smiled Sir Francis, feeling the bittersweet feeling of a father whose child has just surpassed them.

George was overjoyed and punched the air, and screamed with delight.

"I understand that he is deservedly pleased but I think he is taking it to the extreme." thought Sir Francis.

It got worse when George started shouting out to the others "Flora, Henry, Mr. March, come and see. I have beaten Sir Francis again."

"Why that little peasant boy, thinking he has beaten I, Sir Francis Varney. I have passed the decades as he has passed an evening reading the Beano. I have lived for centuries and destroyed all that have come against me. I have..."

Then everyone piled into the parlour and congratulated George, who explained every move in incredible detail. Sir Francis fumed quietly, but his thoughts were anything but quiet.

"Who does he think he is? He gloats over his "Victory" over me. If he wants to see the true meaning of power, then he will see me in all my fury, and he will tremble before me. I should slice his head from his shoulders for such impertinence. In fact why should I not?"

Varney reared up behind the throng of humans, his eyes went red with rage, and he seemed to elongate himself until he towered above them. He looked down and could see that blood pulsing through their veins. He could hear the beats of their hearts. He sniffed, and he could sense their blood type (O, O, B+ and A- by the way, sadly no AB) and even what they had last eaten. He stared at their throats, his eyes flicking from one to the other, looking for the carotid artery that throbbed the most with life. He decided that he should best take Mr. March first, as he was the biggest risk. Then he could take his time feasting on the children. Blood rage filled his mind and he leaned over, reaching out his strong, long fingers to seize hold of the lycan.

"Stop ", the rational part of his mind said "What are you thinking? These are your friends. They have made your long life better than you ever thought it would be. They have treated you as a person, not a monster."

He stopped, mid lunge, and looked down. The others were oblivious to his change, and he slowly shrank back down to his original size, and his eyed stopped glowing.

"What did I nearly do?" he asked himself, and then turned and fled the room, green tears flowing from his eyes.

Chapter Fourteen – Suspicious Minds

The rest of the week was all very strange. Sir Francis seemed to distance himself from the children, still being sociable but not coming too close to them. Little did they suspect that every day, the blood rage was growing inside him, and he was struggling to control it. He was torn between wanting to spend time with his friends, and not wanting to put them at risk.

Flora was still upset, as many of her favourite shiny things (she liked shiny things as much as Henry liked diggers) had been disappearing from her room, or her bag. Even from her hair!

Mr. March was still concerned about his struggles to change back, and it was now getting worse. Every night he dreamt about being a wolf, of hunting through woods, stalking prey, and ripping out their throats. Every morning he awoke, covered in sweat, and half changed back into the great wolf. And he knew, somehow, that if he changed again fully, and soon, then that change may be permanent.

Lycan-kind are not the most, erm, academic of supernatural creatures. They have the attention span of a spaniel, and are too restless to ever really study their unique condition. So Mr. March felt unable to resolve his problem himself. So on the fifth morning since he had remained (mostly) human, he decided to go and see the one person who may be able to help him. Leaving 99 Shackledown early, he headed off into town.

As he went past the local Curry's, he vaguely noticed a display TV on in the window. It was showing the morning's local news, and on the TV a strange man was being interviewed live on air. He had a round face with dull wiry red hair plastered over the top of it. He wore square yellow shaded glasses, and had a wispy moustache, and an attempt at a goatee which was really more just a loose collection of fluff. The scrolling red banner read "Sighted in Bedlamton. Local man claims to have film of extrat…". Mr. March glanced at it, but nothing sunk in, as he was too preoccupied.

He turned down a side alley and was soon at the steps down to a bookshop, although it could be argued that it is "The" bookshop, not that many people were aware of it. Overhead hung a faded sign saying:

"CHARLES HOLLAND: ANTIQUE AND VINTAGE BOOK SHOP", or at least it should have. Instead the sign was very faded, and read:

"ARE LAND ANTI AND VIN AGE BOOSH."

He skipped lightly down the stairs, and through the door. A little bell tingled. As if by magic the shopkeeper did not appear, as he was already behind the counter at the rear of the shop. Mr. March slalomed around the stacks of books and arrived at the counter without knocking any over (for once)

Behind the counter, the man glanced up over his pince nez glasses, and smiled thinly and said "Ah, Mr. M. Is it Wodensday already? Time for our little game?"

"Sadly not, Mr. H, it is Fritagday. I was hear two days ago, remember."

"Ah, yes. I do so lose track of time, you know?"

Mr. March nodded to his friend, Mr. Holland.

"I seem to have a problem."

"A conundrum, very good! One does so like a puzzle – but I do not have too much time. I am expecting a delegation from Archive 8 to land shortly. So we best make haste - shall we retire into the back?"

"If we must. But don't get out of my sight. You know what happened last time."

"Indeed, Mr. M, I will be your guide."

T

hey disappeared, not literally, but instead behind the curtain behind the desk. Once more Mr. March was in The Archives. He hated The Archives.

Mr. H confidently negotiated his way through the maze of bookshelves and corridors. Mr. March followed closely behind, not taking his eye off his friend. The Archives was immense, and far too large to fit into the rear of Mr. H's shop. Mr. March knew that The Archive didn't actually exist in the human world, but was somewhere in a separate plane of existence. Mr. H had tried to explain it once and it had made Mr. March's head ache.

Finally, after about 15 minutes, they arrived at an oak door. Mr. H opened it and walked through it into a comfortable, if old fashioned, study. He seated himself down in a wingback leather armchair, and signaled for Mr. March to sit in its twin, opposite. Somehow a silver tray was already on the table between. On the tray was a china tea service, and Mr. H picked up the ornately painted teapot, and poured tea into both of the cups. It was piping hot. He then added a spot of milk and mixed them with a silver tea spoon. He handed a cup, on its saucer of course, to Mr. March.

"Right, now we are comfortable and refreshed, what is your puzzle?"

Mr. March explained to Mr. H the difficulties he had recently had when changing back to human, and the dreams he was having. Mr. H stayed silent, eyes closed, as he listened. When Mr. March had finished, his eyes flicked back open.

"Some questions, if I may. So you say you are spending more time in wolf form than ever before. Correct?"

Mr. March nodded.

"Mainly so that you do not disappoint this boy, Henry?"

"Yes."

"And now you have decided to stay in human form for a week? But you think that these dreams are trying to suggest to you that you should turn back to your lupine form? Interesting. Very interesting. Any changes to your diet?"

"Nope."

"Any new clothes."

"Do I look like I have new clothes?"

"Indeed not, but one has to check."

"Anything new you are wearing?"

"Well, only my collar."

"Collar?"

"Yes like a dog's collar. The children suggested I wear it when in wolf form in case I am seen by any other humans – so I look more dog-like."

"You, a lycan? Wearing a collar fashioned for a cockapoo or a sprocker? Ridiculous. But by any chance are you wearing it now?"

"No, of course not, I only wear it in my other form. I think I have it in my bag. I wanted to get new dog tags for it."

"Dog tags? They have really tamed the beast, have they not? But still, can I see this item."

"Yes of course". Mr. March rummaged in his satchel and found the collar and handed it to Mr. H. who examined it closely. He stared at it through his pince nez, and then, rather surprisingly, sniffed it.

"Where did you get this collar from?"

"Henry gave it to me as a present."

"Indeed.", Mr. H stood up and walked to a nearby bookshelf and removed a large hardback volume. He sat back down, and turned the pages until he found what he was looking for.

"Aha. Attend here, Mr. M.", he said, placing the book on his desk. Mr. March stood and walked over and started at a picture of a flower. A tall, purple-blue flower.

"*Aconitum Napellus*. Do you recognize it?"

March shook his head.

"It's a flower of the *Ranunculales* order. It's also known as Devil's Helmet, Monkshood, Blue rocket, and…..Wolfsbane. It's a deadly poison to humans, and normal wolves, and is believed by some to have been the poison that killed Socrates, not Hemlock. But it is not deadly to lycan, but has other interesting effects."

"Such as?"

"If a lycan is exposed to it too often, and it gets into their blood, then they will try to turn permanently into a wolf, or if in lycan form, will not want to turn back to human. You have a good nose, smell your collar."

Mr. March picked up the collar and sniffed it. It smelt faintly of something sweet and aromatic.

"Your collar is impregnated with a concentrated potion of Wolfsbane. It is permeating your skin, when you wear it, and entering your blood stream. It is said, that it will make a man turn into a lycan, when the wolfsbane blooms, and the moon is bright. Is the moon not currently bright?"

"Yes, not quite full, but high and bright. It turns full in a couple of days."

"Well, it would seem that if you had continued to wear this, then sometime, possibly at full moon, you would either turn into your lycan form, or remain in it, forever."

Mr. March stared in shock at Mr. H.

"It would appear, my friend, that someone wants you to be a wolf, and only a wolf. The main question is whom."

"Not Henry?"

"He would be the logical suspect."

"But he's only six. How would he know? And how would he be able to prepare a deadly poison without hurting himself? And where did he get the flowers from? They aren't local."

"Indeed. There are a lot more questions to fathom, but don't forget, as I once told my dear friend Sir Arthur many years ago, "When you have eliminated the impossible, whatever remains, however improbable, must be the truth.""

Chapter Fifteen – CODE RED!

Back at Ratpole House, the three kids were lounging around, rather appropriately, in the lounge. Henry was bored as there was no Mr. March, or more importantly, Maximus, to play with. Flora was still upset at the loss of her shiny things. George was puzzled as to why Sir Francis was keeping his distance from them all.

Sir Francis sat at the far side of the room, as far as he could from the children, but he could still smell their blood. He stared down at the floor, gloomily, and unsure of what to do. He couldn't tell them to leave, as they may never return. He couldn't tell them what he was thinking, as they may get scared, and then never return. So he just sat there, looking glum, trying not to breathe through his nose (which was actually quite easy as he didn't need to breathe).

George muttered to himself, "That's enough. I'm sick of this. Something is wrong and I will find out what."

He swung his feet down off the sofa and stood up, quickly, and walked over to Sir Francis.
"I have had enough of this, Sir Francis. Why are you avoiding us? Why are you ignoring us? What have we done?" George demanded.

"Nothing, dear boy, but please stand back. You are too close."

George's throat was at eye level with Varney, who could only focus on the steady pulse of blood, and the beat of George's heart.

"Why am I too close? Are we not good enough for you anymore?" shouted George, furiously.

"You do not understand, dear boy, it is nothing to do with you."

"Then what is it?" George demanded, grabbing hold of Sir Francis' cold hand in frustration.

Varney flinched back at the touch, but one of his long fingernails accidentally caught the back of George's hand, scouring a mark in it several inches long. Then a crimson line appeared in the cut.

Varney stared at the wound in horror, his eyes widened and turned the same shade as the blood.

"Get back, George. Get back now. You are in very grave danger."

"But…"

"But me no buts, get back NOWWWWWWWWWWW!"

But it was too late. All thought left Sir Francis' head, as the blood rage filled him. He stood up, and loomed over George, who finally had the sense to step back. But not far enough. A long arm shot out and grabbed George by the shoulder in a grip as firm as a vice and as cold as death.

Varney seemed to grow in height, and his red eyes glowed hypnotically. He opened his mouth and his lips drew back from his long fangs. He looked like a cobra about to strike at its prey

George was terrified, as he had never seen Sir Francis like this, but he managed to keep his wits. Just.

"CODE RED" he shouted, reaching for his pocket. His free hand closed around a cold metal object. Flora and Henry were up from the sofas in double quick time. They ran towards George, also reaching for something in their pockets.

Varney moved in to strike at George, a terrible lust filling his eyes. As he lunged towards George, he was faced by a shimmering silver item. George held up the crucifix in front of him, and Flora and Henry were either side of him, holding up their crosses. Varney hissed, and drew back, releasing George.

George had made a contingency plan. He liked making contingency plans, and he had seen Superman 4 and a few episodes of Buffy to

know that sometimes that the good can go bad. So they had all agreed to always carry a cross in case Sir Francis ever reverted to his previous life.

They advanced on Varney, who drew back into the corner, fear and hate spread across his face. They had him trapped. The vampyr hissed at them as they advanced, but was unable to escape. He seemed to climb up the wall, backwards, until he was wedged between the wall and the ceiling, staring down at them. Devoid of other options, Varney concentrated and summoned the image of a mischief of rats, and then he started to change into them.

Except he didn't. The glood obviously was still in his body, and instead of a group of brown rodents, he turned into a colony of bunny rabbits. Green dwarf eared rabbits, to be exact. They sat there, noses twitching, staring up at the Bannerworths. They didn't look hugely threatening with their small floppy ears, buck teeth instead of fangs, and twitching noses.

"Oh no" thought Varney to all of him selves, as his mind was split across all the green rabbits. It was a very discombobulating feeling.

"Stop him, or them, from escaping" cried George. He was worried that if Varney managed to escape, then he would go on a bloody rampage and no one would be safe. However, the rabbits were surprisingly fast, and tried to break the determined line of the three children.

One tried to get past George, who raised a foot and kicked it back. It squealed as it flew back into the corner.

"You kicked a rabbit, George, that's mean", said Flora.

"It's not a rabbit, it's part of Sir Francis"

"Oh, I suppose", admitted Flora, as one tried to dart past her. She shrugged, and kicked it back into the corner. It squeaked in annoyance and frustration when it landed. The room was in chaos as the children tried to run around and stop the bunnies from escaping. But there was only three of them, and there were more than a dozen rabbits. First one got through the human barricade, then a second, and soon the others were finding gaps as the children tired.

Once a few had got through, the floodgates opened, and a stream of green bunnies lolloped past the tired kids, who were helpless to stop them. They fled up the stairs, hopping up, their round tails twitching. At the top of the stairs, Varney reformed himself, his rage dissipating. He felt only sadness and sorrow that he had tried to hurt his friends.

He turned dramatically, coat flaring out like a cape, to walk off, and almost fell over. He cursed, and caught himself on the bannister, and looked down. He was missing the bottom half of his left leg. He looked down and saw a single bunny still hopping up the stairs. There was always one. He waited impatiently until the rabbit reached him and was incorporated back into his body.

He sighed and then turned and floated upstairs to hide in his room.

Chapter Sixteen – Betrayals

George, Flora and Henry fled Ratpole House. They burst through the door, and down the twisty turny path to the gate, and flung it open. Chili, who had missed all the action as he had been sleeping in the kitchen, followed moments later, chittering excitedly. Then they stood there, on the pavement, breathing heavily.

"What do we do now?" asked Flora.

"What happened to Sir Francis?" asked Henry.

"I don't know, I don't know", snapped George, more in irritation that for once he didn't know what to do. He gathered his thoughts.

"Look, it's still daytime, let's go back home and see if we can find Mr. March and see if he has any ideas. But whatever we do, don't tell mother."

Flora and Henry nodded. If mother/ mummy / mama knew they would never be allowed around Ratpole House again. Not that they wanted to go there at the moment.

They walked quickly to 99 Shackledown Road, and unlocked the door and walked in. Little did they know that standing in a side alley opposite was a tall man, with a wide brimmed hat and a long coat.

"One down, two to go", he muttered to himself, nearly but not quite smiling. Things were progressing well.

Back in the house, mother was still at work, which was a relief. Mr. March wasn't in his room, which was unusual. So they searched around, shouting,

"Mr. March, we need you. Something terrible has happened."

No one replied. They searched the house. They arrived at Henry's room and opened the door. They were surprised to see Mr. March sat on Henry's bed, holding a book.

"Mr. March, we need your help-"

"How could you?" he asked without looking up, "Was it all of you? Henry? George? Flora? Or was it just Henry?"

"What do you mean, Mr. M?" asked Henry, clearly upset.

Mr. March threw the book at George, who caught it. It was entitled *"Flora and fauna and their powers over supernatural and mythical creatures"*. He recognised the book. It had seen a copy in the library in Ratpole House.

"Turn to page 54."

George flicked through the pages, and round it. The page was entitled *"Aconitum Napellus"*, and it was a recipe for making a tincture with the flowers. George read silently. The ingredients and method were underlined in various coloured marker pens – the same coloured pens that lay on Henry's desk. It detailed how to make a potion that would keep a lycan in wolf form, permanently.

"I checked your eBay account, the one you are using to buy the various ingredients for the glood. Look what I found."

He pointed as a printed sheet of A4. George was quite surprised that Mr. March knew how to use a printer. On it was the details of an eBay transaction from a couple of weeks ago.

"Henry, I know you like me best as a wolf, but how could you try to trap me in that form?" Mr. March asked the little boy.

"I didn't, Mr. M. Honest", tears filled Henry's eyes.

"Then how do you account that this solution was on the inside of the collar. The very collar you gave me that I have been wearing like a tame mutt?" Mr. March shouted "I trusted you all, I loved you all, and you try to turn me into a pet pooch. I am of lycan born. We stand in both worlds."

"But Mr. M.", stuttered Henry, tears now flowing openly down his face.

"No more. I don't know whether it was all of you, or just Henry, but I never want to see you again. And if I do, you will regret it", he growled, staring at them with wild yellow eyes.

Without a further word, he pushed past them and fled down the stairs. They heard the door slam closed. Flora hugged poor Henry, whilst George stood apart, thinking.

Outside, the tall figure in the alley saw Mr. March storm out of number 99, and slam the door closed. He marched over the road and down towards Ratpole House.

"Two", he murmured.

When Mrs. Bannerworth returned less than an hour later, she was surprised to find all the children at home. Henry was in his room, and apparently didn't want to be disturbed. Flora and George sat at the kitchen table, talking through how their lives had turned upside down in the last hour. Chili sat on Flora's shoulder, chittering to himself.

"Hi, guys", said Mrs. Bannerworth. She came into the kitchen, put down her bags, and opened a window. Then she turned the oven on to start cooking. She turned around and looked at them. They both smiled up at her, weakly. "Hmm, something wrong? You don't seem too happy?"

George shook his head almost negligibly but Flora noticed.

"Nothing mummy, just a busy day and we are all a bit tired."

"Where's Henry?"

"Upstairs in his room, having a nap."

"My, he must be tired. Oh, whilst you mention rooms, your little friend's cage is starting to smell a bit. Can you clean it out please?"

"But mummy-"

"Now please, before tea."

"OK", said Flora, and she glumly headed for the stairs with Chili.

"Right, George. I know somethings going on. Henry's not asleep, I could hear crying from his window when I was at the door. Flora looks concerned, and I have never known you so quiet. What is going on?"

George thought fast. He decided that he would have to give some information or mother would not let it go. Anything about Sir Francis was too inflammatory and risky, so he decided to stay closer to home.

"It's Mr. March. He's left us. We had an argument and he shouted at us and stormed out."

"Ah, that explains Henry. What about Flora?"

"She's just upset as well. We all liked Mr. March."

"There's something else, George. Your nostrils are flaring. They always do that when you tell a lie."

"But it's not a lie."

"No, but it's not the whole truth is it?"

George was starting to sweat a bit. His mother was very perceptive, and he was under pressure to tell more.

"Well, Sir-"

But there was a cry from upstairs, and he heard Flora shouting "WHY YOU LITTLE GREEN TRAITOR, IT WAS YOU ALL ALONG!"

And there was a crash of furniture, and then Chili came scampering down the stairs as if his tail was on fire, closely followed by Flora, who's face was red with fury. Chili got to the door, which was closed, but spotted the open window and jumped out of it.

Flora stopped in the middle of the kitchen, screaming "THE LITTLE RAT FACED......."

"Calm down, dear, what's happened?"

Flora could hardly speak she was so apoplectic. She pointed upstairs. They all went up to her room and she pointed at Chili's cage. On the floor, in the corner, were a couple of old cushions that served as his bed. Mrs. Bannerworth reached in, and took one. It was heavy. She found the zip to the cover, and rooted around inside. Her hand came out holding several shimmering objects.

"My bracelet. Your necklace….your-", she stopped and turned "So Chili has been stealing from us?" she asked of Flora.

Flora just nodded.

Outside, the tall figure watched in satisfaction, as he saw the small green squirrel climb down the outside of the window. Chili stood on the pavement outside number 99, his eyes wide in shock. He chittered to himself, a sad, lonely noise. Then he shrugged and scampered over to the only other place he knew he may still be welcome – Ratpole House.

"Three. Stage one: Segregation, complete." He ticked this off on his plan.

He reached into one of the deep pockets of the duster coat and pulled out a very old mobile phone. The kind that slid open and used to be cool in the 90's, especially if you were wearing a long black coat and sunglasses. He dialed a number, and it was soon picked up.

"You're up", and then hung up.

"Stage two initiated. Exposure", Earthborn whispered. He permitted himself a brief half smile. "All too easy", he thought.

Chapter Seventeen – The Art of War

Mr. March stood in the entrance hall of Ratpole House, shouting "Sir Francis, where are you?"

No reply. He checked the lounge, the kitchen, the parlour. No sign of him. So he headed upstairs, right to the top of the western tower – towards Sir Francis bed chamber. He arrived at the door, and pushed it open. The room was dark, no surprise, but Mr. March had excellent night vision. He picked out a shape in the corner. It was Varney.

He was sat on the floor, knees pulled up to his chin, arms around his legs, as if he was hugging himself. He was rocking from side to side and moaning.

"Sir Francis, what's happened?"

"I do not quite know, Maximus. I was overcome by the blood rage like I have rarely felt it before. I attacked George, and was intent on drinking him and the other children dry. Fortunately, they were prepared, and fought me off. Such clever children . . . .", he tailed off.

"You what?" exclaimed Mr. March "but you've drunk nothing but glood since you woke."

"Apart from a couple of rats when I first awakened. Nothing since, I swear. And that was months ago.."

"I thought the children looked upset"

"You have seen them? Are the in good health? Did they mention me?"

"I only saw them briefly, but…..", Mr. March fell silent.

"What Maximus?"

"I had evidence that Henry, and maybe George, were using Wolfsbane to try to turn me into a wolf. Permanently. I confronted them. I was angry. There was shouting, and then I left", he finished sadly.

"Something is amiss here. Let us go to the parlour to contemplate our options. There may be another agency at work here."

They headed down the stairs, and had only been in the parlour for a short while when they heard a noise in the hallway. They went to investigate, and saw the cat flap was swinging, and in the centre of the hall was Chili, chittering excitedly.

"Hmmm, what ails the erstwhile professor?" mused Sir Francis. "Can you interpret?"

"I can make out some of what he is saying. He says "Flora, theft, bad Chili". I think he means that Flora accused him of theft and is angry with him."

"So, happenstance it is clearly not? What is the likelihood that I attack George, you blame Henry, and Flora accuses the good professor, all on the same day, within hours? This has been orchestrated. It is a tactic as old as time. When faced with a superior force, what do you do?"

"Try to split them up?"

"Exactly. Sun Tzu. The Art of War. Our forces have been halved. We are here in Ratpole, they are in number 99. We must inform the children. They may be the target of these machinations."

"We need proof. Broken trust is hard to repair, especially when tempers are frayed."

"True, good Maximus. Clear heads must prevail."

They went to go back into the parlour, Mr. March picking up the clearly upset Chili and placing him on his shoulder. Before they made it, there was a thump on the door.

"The evening paper, no doubt."

Sir Francis has recently subscribed to the Bedlamton Gazette, the local newspaper. He claimed to get it for current affairs, although everyone knew he always turned to the obituaries first, then the house prices, and then the crossword. Sighing, Mr. March walked over to the door, and opened it. He picked up the paper and stared down in horror.

"Oh no", he exclaimed.

Chapter Eighteen – Foul Brews

Meanwhile, back at Number 99, things had settled down into a dread silence. The kids sat around the kitchen table, staring glumly at their food (which George thought was an enchilada, Flora thought was a cannelloni, and Henry thought was just "blurgh"). They all pushed it around their plate with their forks, showing no interest in actually placing any of it even close to their mouths.

Mrs. Bannerworth stood and watched them, her heart going out to each of them. They were all so different. George, who could normally solve any problem with logic and reason. Flora who lived on instinct, and Henry who thrived on enthusiasm. All were sitting there with faces longer than the average horse. Or a pony in Henry's case.

Mrs. Bannerworth had managed to get little from them. She was aware that something had happened between the kids and Sir Francis. She also had deduced that Henry had argued with Mr. March. And she knew that Flora was hurting from betrayal due to Chili's apparent light-fingeredness. Or light-clawdness, if that was even a word. Which it wasn't. However she was short on detail about everything else.

She resorted to what most British people do in a time of crisis. She boiled the kettle and made a cup of tea. In fact, she went even further and made a pot of tea. She had the feeling that it would be a three cup problem. She slightly regretted her plans for a bubble bath with bubbles, but that would have to wait.

The kettle boiled, or in fact she stopped it just before it boiled ("To boil is to spoil", as her dad used to say). She poured a bit of the nearly-but-not-quite boiled water into the tea pot, and swilled it around. How much a bit of water was is not known, but it was just to warm the pot. She tipped the bit of water out, and then she added a couple of tea bags of, well, tea, popped the lid on and let it stew.

She absently counted to herself in her head (count to 180, then pour). When the time was ready, she poured the piping hot (but not boiling hot) tea into a china cup, and added a spot of milk. Much like a bit of water, a spot of milk wasn't a recognised measurement outside of the UK. She stirred them together with a teaspoon and took a sip.

"Ghastly", she thought to herself and shuddered. She hated tea, but it was well known that drinking tea solved problems, and if it was a three cup problem, then it was a difficult problem. Mrs. Bannerworth theorised that she thought better whilst drinking tea, as the unpleasant flavor and aroma made her think quicker so she could solve the problem sooner. Then she could pour the rest of the tea down the plughole and drink something she liked. Like something with bubbles. She liked drinks with bubbles.

She leaned against the work surface, facing the three kids, sipping at the foul brew. She studied each of them. George, as ever, was deep in thought. He was concentrating so hard on what had gone wrong that his tongue was sticking out from between his lips on one side. He only did that when he was in deep thought. Mrs. Bannerworth always thought he looked so cute when he did that, not that she would dare tell him. He also reminded her so much of George's dad, gone far too soon.

Flora was still playing with her food. Or rather she was herding it, as she was pushing the enchilada / cannelloni hybrid in the centre of the plate, until it was almost an animal shape, and then stabbing it several times with her fork. It was not wise to get too close to Flora when she was annoyed and in possession of cutlery.

Henry had found his favourite cuddly toy, Snow Bear, that used to go everywhere with him. Since his discovery of diggers and tractors, Henry spent less and less time with Snow Bear. But now he was in Henry's firm embrace, as Henry hugged him to his face, rubbing his cheek against the fur of the bear. All whilst sucking his thumb. Henry was sucking his own thumb, not the bears. That would have been silly.

Mrs. Bannerworth had never worried about their association with Sir Francis. Coming from a "family" like hers, the supernatural and mystical was not such a mystery to her, and she had done some of her own research behind the scenes. She was not without resources of her own. She had decided that it was safe, or relatively safe.

In her view, nothing was truly safe. Her most terrifying experience of parenthood was when George first learned to ride a bike and they both went into the town centre on their bikes. George first, and then her, whizzing down the hill into the high street. Her heart was in her mouth the whole time – which is pretty inconvenient when you are trying to ride a bike.

She believed that children had to learn to assess risk and grow – and who better to do that than George?

George may have got most of his cold logic from his father, but not all of it, and so Mrs. Bannerworth started to reason her way through things. She also did not believe in coincidences. Everything had a reason, and there were often patterns linking seemingly random events.

From what she could tell, the first incident happened with Sir Francis, which had led the kids to run back here just as Mr. March arrived, seemingly furious at them, especially Henry.

Then, after Mr. March left, shortly after, the discovery of the loot in Chili's cage was discovered. But she specifically asked Flora to clean the cage as soon as she had got in – but why was that? It was because it had started to smell that morning before she went to work, but she hadn't seen Flora to ask her. But oddly enough, Chili's cage had never stunk, even if it had been left for longer. He was quite a considerate creature, only answering nature in one place – much like a human using the bathroom.

So, in one afternoon, George had lost his best friend; Flora had thrown out her best friend; and Henry had his best friend / pet dog walk out on him. So now, her three were here. But where were the other three. Sir Francis would no doubt be at Ratpole, and she assumed Mr. March and Chili would have made for Varney's home as well.

So a team of six had been neatly cut in half, with each half in a different, but nearby location. This was not random. This was planned. But by who?

Pleased that she had figured a lot of that out, and that she may not need another cup of tea, Mrs. Bannerworth looked up. She happened to catch the small TV on the wall in the kitchen, which was on but muted. It was the local news, and she glanced at the red rolling banner, and where the roving reporter was reporting live from.

"Oh my", she said.

Chapter Nineteen – Press Gang

18:12, Ratpole House, the hallway

Mr. March stared down at the newspaper in horror. The headline, in large bold letters, said,

"ALIENS IN BEDLAMTON" and below were several photos. He was aghast when he noticed that they were of the children, and him in wolf form. And even worse than that…..

"Sir Francis, you really need to see this", he shouted, and loped towards the parlour in great bounds.

18:13, Number 99, the kitchen

"ET HAS FOUND A HOME" said the red banner, running across the bottom of the screen. Above that, a reporter called Izzy Necessary was interviewing a rather odd looking man. They were in front of a rather grand old house. One that she recognised all too well.

"George, Flora, Henry. You had better stop pretending to eat, and watch this", she reached for the remote, which was actually further away from the TV than she was (they are not called remote controls for nothing), and clicked the mute button, which was now the un-mute button, to un-mute it.

"And so Mr. Tuesday, when did you first suspect that aliens were living in Bedlamton?"

"Well, Isobel, let me tell you……."

"But that's…….?", said George.

"Yes. I am very much afraid it is", replied Mrs. Bannerworth.

18:14, Ratpole House, the parlour

"But this is impossible!", spluttered Sir Francis, genuinely shocked "This is inconceivable! This is implausible. This is i-."

"Yes indeed", Mr. March agreed, jumping in a bit in the hope that it would stop Sir Francis listing every other word he knew that began with "I".

"This has never happened. It is a well-known fact of vampyr physiology that this is impossible. Much the same as we do not appear in mirrors, and do not cast a shadow. It must be an imitation."

"My thoughts as well, but from reading on through, it seems they have been independently substantiated - or the paper would not have published them."

"But this is impossible, inconceivable, implausible, improbable", reverted Sir Francis, managing to sneak in a new "I" word.

Mr. March shrugged his shoulders, and hoped that Sir Francis would stop ranting soon. As they had a very real problem, and may be in very real danger.

18:15, Number 99, the kitchen, staring intently at the TV

"But that's Ratpole House" blurted out Flora.

"On TV", chipped in Henry.

"And it's live now!", shouted George, half in excitement, half in dread.

The three children and Mrs. Bannerworth turned as one and stared at the front door. They crossed to it, and Mrs. Bannerworth turned the handle and opened it.

"Oh my" she repeated. In her mind she thought something else completely but didn't dare say it in front of the kids.

Outside, the whole of the street was lit up.

18:15, Ratpole House, still the parlour, staring at the local rag

"How have they done it, Maximus? How has someone been able to take a daguerreotype of me?"

"Erm, most people call them photographs, or photos now, Sir Francis."

"Oh pish posh, you know I like not this new slang. But how?"

"Well it seems very strange. It's a black and white photo. I am in black and white, as are the kids, and Chili. And the park, and the birds, and the pond. But you, your skin is blue. Well it is in the ones they have of you after you changed back in the park."

"So does that mean that we have been compromised?"

"It would appear likely."

"Will they know where we live?"

"Possibly, or more like probably."

"Oh, we are in a pretty pickle."

Then they heard a lot of noise outside. They went to the door and pulled it open. Outside it was bedlam in Bedlamton. Or in Shackledown Road anyway.

18:16, Number 99, outside the front door

"Look at that. There are people everywhere….", gasped Flora.

"And they are all down the road…." continued Henry.

"Outside Ratpole House", concluded George.

As they looked down the street all they could see was a mass of people. People with signs that read "Beam ME up, Scotty", "I believe", "The force is with ME."

At the front, right outside the gate to Ratpole House, were a number of news vans. Lights illuminated the tall stone wall, and in front of it stood various people, some wearing terrible ties and suits, and all carrying microphones. They spoke into them, staring at the camera, as the pictures were relayed live around the world. Or at least live to Bedlamton.

"What do we do?" asked Henry.

"Go and have a look, I suppose", said George, shrugging.

18:17, Ratpole House, outside the green front door

"What are all these mortals doing outside? Is it an angry mob of peasants?"

18:12

18:13

18:14

18:15

18:16

18:17

"We don't use the word peasants these days, Sir Francis."

"Oh. Serfs?"

"No. Try again."

"Erm, Thrall? Servant? Vassal?"

"No. No twice. And No thrice!"

"Oh, is "townsfolk" OK?"

"Yes, much better."

"But where are their pitchforks and their burning torches?"

"They seem to have swapped them for smartphones and selfie sticks."

"Really? No style these days. Back in the olden days, I used to have angry mobs try to burn me out at least once a decade. I used to think of it as a "meet the neighbours" kind of event. Incidentally, that is how village barbeques were invented."

"Well, Sir Francis, I don't think they suspect you are a vampire-"

"Vampyr, rhymes with-"

"This is hardly the time", Mr. March snapped back, uncharacteristically.

"My apologies, Maximus. Some habits die hard."

"Well, unless you want us to die hard, then maybe we had best concentrate on events at hand."

"I think I am about to have a very bad day", said Sir Francis dramatically

"Night."

"Apologies again, Maximus, bad night. Too many movies on demand."

"But as I was saying, they don't suspect you are undead."

"Or not dead. Nosferatu means not dead"

"Please, will you stop it? They seem to think you are not of this earth."

"What? I definitely am! All vampyr's are reborn from the very earth that they are buried in…."

"Just listen! They seem to think that you are an alien. From another planet."

"Ah, I see, from Mars? What are the chances of that?"

"A lot less than a million to 1 it seems", sighed Mr. March.

18:17, Outside Ratpole House, in the crowd

The Bannerworths and their mum threaded their way through the crowd. All around them, people were waving banners and placards, and chanting,

"E.T, E.T, E.T.,
Come out and meet me, me, me"

(It wasn't a very good chant!)

They all seemed to favour dressing in cagoules or anoraks and a lot had cameras around their necks. The majority of conspiracy theorists believed that smartphones were controlled by the government, and so they didn't trust them. But they still used them as they were so useful for googlemaps and

Wikipedia. Not that they trusted googlemaps or Wikipedia either (as they were obviously controlled by the government, or "a" government, they just weren't sure which one).

By a mixture of dexterity, fleetness of foot and brute force, the four Bannerworths managed to get near the front of the crowd. The main news groups were currently back to interviewing the red haired fellow in glasses that they had seen on the TV moments earlier. Ray Thursday or something.

"Well, as I said earlier, my suspicions were first aroused when I was doing some detailed original research…."

"Searching on the internet, I bet", thought George. George didn't consider googling stuff as real research.

"…into strange sightings in the local area. They all centred on this street and so I did some in depth surveillance. Then I noticed the strange person that seemed to reside in this very residence. Further research identified that the same person had been registered as living here for 200 years, which is obviously impossible…"

"Bit sloppy there, Sir Francis", George thought.

"…and so I came to the only logical conclusion. That the resident of the house was a-"

"Vampire?", asked one of the reporters. Everyone laughed.

"Don't be so ridiculous. Such a thing does not exist", harrumphed Thursday, or was it Tuesday?. "No, not a vampire…"

"*Vampyr*" thought George, unable to stop himself.

"But a visitor from another-"

"LOOK UP THERE" shouted someone in the crowd and pointed.

Everyone stopped and looked. At the top of the drive, now visible as the garden was nice and tidy and the trees had been trimmed back, was the green door of Ratpole House. It was opening…

Chapter Twenty – Tunnels and Tolls

At the top of the hill, Sir Francis and Mr. March stood transfixed. Well, Mr. March did. He had never had a mob of townsfolk staring at him. Unless you count the time that he mistook the window of Debenhams as a good place to have a kip when he changed back from his lupine form.

Sir Francis looked down at the masses of people. Masses was a slight exaggeration, or in truth a very big exaggeration. Bedlamton was not a large town, and there were about 80-100 people milling around. Sir Francis could see news vans, reporters and cameras. A seeming sea of smartphones on long poles were pointing at him (although smartphones themselves are not very pointy), with their flashes blinking and flashing back at him. The spotlights from the news vans were trained on him until the doorway was lit up as if it was noon.

Sir Francis hissed and raised his arm and recoiled from the light, using his jacket as a cape. He backed away into the doorway. Below, someone shouted and pointed. Then another shouted,

"Look, we can see him, but he's not showing up on our video cameras. How is this possible?"

"I indeed found the same. They have based their deflector technology on 21st century technology. They had forgotten the power of 1970's machinery – as I can still take photographs of the creatures with my good old Pentax. But enough talk. Time for action", shouted Tuesday.

Tuesday, who was normally quite timid when it came to personal danger, was emboldened by the crowd, who were fast transitioning into a mob.

"With me all", he shouted.

And then Tuesday ran and jumped over the wall into the garden. What actually happened was he ran into the wall, rather than jump it. He then managed to clamber up to the top of the four foot wall, and proceeded to get stuck. His arms and head were over the wall, whereas his legs were still on the other side. He gasped and demanded someone help. With an unceremonious push on his round rump, he was pushed over the wall, where he landed in a crumpled heap, upside down.

Sir Francis watched in horror. Up until then , the crowd had remained on the street. But with one person entering the garden it was like a dam bursting. First a trickle of people jumped the wall, and then some bright spark thought it was much easier just to open the gate.

With the gate open, the trickle became a flood, and the sea of people was getting closer, starting to move up the twisty turny path like an incoming tide. Then Sir Francis got sick of water metaphors and decided that there were just a lot of people on his land and this could get dangerous – but for whom he was not entirely sure.

He pulled Mr. March, who was frozen in amazement, back into the house and slammed the green door closed. He used such force that the old piano behind it tinkled briefly. He concentrated and spoke with his mind to Ratpole House, asking it to do what it could to stop the torrent of people. Oh blast, he thought, another water metaphor.

Instantaneously, all the locks in the house clicked shut. Window shutters closed and bolted themselves. A change came over the old house. Since it had been renovated, the outside had been light and welcoming. But now, the house pulled into itself and tried to surround itself in shadows. The pale walls became dark and scary. The trees and rose bushes seemed to grow and lean over towards the house, and across the path, giving it a kind of wall of thorns. Even the sky above seemed to darken, and storm clouds seemed to gather above. Even the high powered flood lights of the news crews seemed to be dampened. The light that flooded in from the lamps seemed to get swallowed up. The whole house went into what can only be described as "INTIMIDATION" mode.

It worked to some degree, as almost everyone on the path stopped and stared. At the front, Tuesday shouted,

"See I told you, it has some sort of deflector shield that's trying to cut off the light and stop us from entering. But nothing will stop us from exposing The Truth".

He said The Truth exactly like that, as if it should be capitalised.

The crowd was now definitely a mob, and started to charge towards the green door.

Inside, Sir Francis and Mr. March ran towards the parlour. Mr. March whistled, a wolf whistle of course. Chili came running, or scampering, towards him and climbed up his leg. Mr. March flinched as the little claws dug into his skin, but then Chili was perched on his shoulder.

They got into the parlour, and Ratpole House slammed the door behind them and locked it.

"Over here", pointed Sir Francis, with one very long, pale finger.

In front of him was a tall inglenook fireplace, tall enough to fit a person standing. He walked into it, and beckoned Mr. March and Chili. Then he rubbed away some of the soot at the back of the chimney until he found what he was looking for. It was a small hole, only a couple of centimeters wide. Again using his incredibly long finger, he stuck it into the hole. There was a shudder, and a grinding noise, and then all of a sudden the floor of the fireplace started to turn.

"A priest-hole?", asked Mr. March.

"Priests had nothing to do with it, thank you very much. I built it myself", Varney said proudly.

"Yourself? Really?"

"Well, to be totally accurate I mesmerized some local builders to install it a few years ago."

"When?"

"Oh about 1782 I think. Secret passages were very de rigeur back then. I had almost forgotten it existed."

"And what happened to the builders afterwards."

"I treated them to a meal and drinks."

"You had them as drinks for a meal, more like"

Sir Francis shrugged, and almost looked embarrassed, but by then the fireplace had turned exactly 180 degrees, and they found themselves in a narrow stone passage.

"Where do we go now?" whispered Mr. March. As he was in a secret passage he felt like it was only appropriate to whisper.

"This heads down though the hill that Ratpole House is built on, and comes out in some old Roman catacombs under the town." explained Sir Francis, not whispering at all. Stone several feet thick surrounded them.

Bedlamton was built on the site of an old Roman fort, and catacombs had been discovered that crisscrossed underneath the town. The full extent of them has never been explored due to poor repair, fallen in tunnels, and lack of funding.

"So we head down", said Mr. March, ominously and in a quiet voice. Again, rather for effect, as he felt it was appropriate.

"Yeessss, down into the deep dark depths of the earth, and into the evils of history"

"Stop trying to be scary. It's not working", lied Mr. March. Chili sat quivering on his shoulder – and not with the cold.

"You really are taking all the fun out of this, Maximus"

The passage was narrow and so they could only walk in single file. There was little light, but that was not the issue as Sir Francis was re-born of the dark, and Mr. March had excellent night vision. The passage seemed to be cold and dry, and warm and humid at the same time, and it twisted its way down through the hill-side. Mr. March hoped they would soon get to the Roman section – as at least they knew how to build straight roads.

Shortly after that, the descent did indeed level off, and the corridor widened and straightened. Then they emerged into a large antechamber. A combination of Doric and Ionic columns were at each side of the rectangular chamber, supporting the tall roof. The floor was a glorious mosaic of coloured stone and glass, featuring images of Jupiter, Neptune, Bacchus and Diana, amongst others.

"Wow, this must be a Roman villa. It's the most complete I have ever heard of. Does anyone else know it's here?" asked Mr. March

"Of course not, Maximus, it would hardly serve as a secret passage if everyone knew about it. All that knew of it are long dead."

"Not all", said a quiet voice from behind them.

With unnatural speed, Sir Francis and Mr. March spun on their heels. Emerging out of the shadows was a tall figure, wearing a wide brimmed hat, pulled down over his eyes, and a long coat. He slowly walked out of the dark, and took off his long coat. He stood there dressed in cowboy boots, black jeans, a sheepskin vest and a blue shirt. A neckerchief was tied around his neck. He picked up a long object that was leaning against the wall, and walked forward. It was a long sword. He advanced, holding the sword loosely in his left hand. It glimmered in the faint light.

"Welcome, Sir Francis Varney. I am delighted to finally make your acquaintance, but not for long. Prepare to meet your doom", said Earthborn, smiling thinly.

Chapter Twenty One – Revelations

George, Flora and Henry watched in dismay as the mob started up the hill towards Ratpole House.

"Well, what do we do now, George?" asked Henry.

"And more to the point, why should we care?" asked Flora "have you all forgotten that our so-called friends betrayed each of us?"

George indicated they should move a bit away from the group of people so they were not overheard.

"Of course not Flora, but something's not right", continued George.

Mrs. Bannerworth stood and watched, not speaking. She could see from the look in George's eyes that he was working his way through the problem. George liked problems, just as Flora liked shiny things and Henry liked diggers. She would only help if he was truly stuck, as she didn't want to take away his big moment. At times like this he looks so much like Daniel, she thought.

"Think, all of you. All summer we were as happy as a pig in muck", said George, inadvertently using one of his dad's favorite sayings, then carried on, "Sir Francis had stopped eating-"

"Drinking."

"Yes, thank you, Henry. Drinking people." he cast a look at mother, as he was aware that he was revealing things that they had never told her before. Mrs. Bannerworth appeared to be absently examining her fingernails and not really playing attention.

"Mr. March was happy splitting his time between human and, erm, his other form. And Chili wouldn't do anything to upset you Flora. He is devoted to you"

"Well of course he is. I am very devotable."

George ignored that, as he didn't have time to give Flora an English lesson.

"Then there's all this", gestured Henry at all the TV cameras and people.

"Precisely, Henry. If one of these things had happened in a day, fine. Even two, I don't like coincidences but I could accept it. But for everything to happen in one day, then I am beyond doubt....."

"Good boy. You are nearly there" thought Mrs. Bannerworth, still pretending to inspect her nails and pretending not to listen.

"Someone, or something, is working against us."

"But who?"

"Whom."

"Sorry, but whom?" asked Henry

"Sticks and Stones, I bet", cried Flora excitedly. "It would be just like them."

"I am not so sure. Or if they are they are only the muscle, not the mastermind. And they signed that contract not to harm us."

"True, but I am sure they would try to wriggle out of it", said Henry

"I don't think Sticks looked to have the capability to organise all this. Last time we saw him he was struggling to stop a crow picking him apart, bit by bit."

The children all smiled briefly at that thought.

"So how do we find out?" asked Flora

"We need to find evidence. We need to get back into Ratpole House" reasoned George.

"But how? Look at all the people that are surrounding it", said Henry.

"Yes, but we know the house, and more importantly-"

"The house knows us!", completed Flora.

"Exactly!"

"Then, let's go!" shouted Henry, raising his arm and charging towards Ratpole House.

George sighed and Flora rolled her eyes at Henry's enthusiasm, but then they charged after him. Mrs. Bannerworth watched them run off, a small smile on her lips. Then she turned and headed home. It was time for a bath, she thought.

Chapter Twenty Two – Half Man, Half dog Biscuit

Mr. March was the first to re-act. He drew himself up and roared,

"If you want him, you will first have to deal with me", and then he started to change. His jaw elongated, and his teeth grew in length and sharpness. Hair, or fur, started to grow from his forehead and cheeks. His body started to stretch, his back widening, ripping his tweed jacket. His legs grew longer and thinner, whilst his arms seemed to elongate as well, to almost match the legs. His suit continued to rip and tear as a wolf started to emerge from it.

However, whilst he was between man and wolf, the stranger darted forward and slashed with the sword. It caught Mr. March on the forearm, and the skin parted under the razor sharp blade. Mr. March drew back his arm and yowled, although the injury was merely a scratch. But then he stopped still.

"What's happening", he asked in a guttural voice, as his vocal cords were half human, half wolf. **"I cannot change, either to wolf or man. What devilry is this?"**

"Devilry? No. Just science, mongrel. My blade is made of Argentium, and that very metal is now in your blood. Only in tiny amounts – but enough", laughed the man. It was a dry laugh, with no humour in it.

"Silver?", said Mr. March, shocked.

"Indeed, or a stronger alloy of it. But more to the point, you will be unable to change whilst it is in your blood. My mission does not include your demise, and so I suggest you quiver in the corner like the craven cur you are."

The wolf-man howled in anger.

"Never. I will always fight to protect my pack", and with that Max (the Maximus / Mr. March hybrid) clad only in a pair of shredded trousers, launched himself at the stranger.

Max did not have the full strength of his lycan form, but he was still stronger and faster than any human. The stranger swung the gleaming sword, and Max ducked and rolled underneath it, rising to his feet inside the reach of the sword. He slashed up with his clawed hand, into the face of the stranger. He cut four deep gouges in the left cheek, but no blood flowed from these wounds. It was as if he had just gouged tracks in the earth.

The stranger smiled, and the gashes in his face knitted back together.

"Your feeble nails will not do much damage to me, I am afraid, you mangy pooch. I was born from the earth. Or, to be true, re-born".

Earthborn swung the great sword, but again Max was too agile to hit. He jumped over the flashing blade, and landed on his hands. Then he flexed his arms, and pushed up. His feet flew forward, followed by the rest of him, and they thudded into the broad chest of Earthborn, who grunted as he was knocked backwards a step. The sword fell to the floor with a clang.

Seeking to press his advantage, Max kicked and dodged, again and again. He was too fast for Earthborn, who couldn't land a blow on Max, and his powerful legs knocked Earthborn back again and again.

Earthborn grunted in frustration, until he was knocked back against one of the tall Doric pillars. He looked groggy and dazed. Max sprang forward, once again launching himself off his hands, so both his long feet raced towards Earthborn's head. Surely one more blow would do it.

But as he was about to hit Earthborn, the tall man reacted. He caught Max's feet in two shovel like hands and spun them round.

Max was in midair, and was in turn spun in midflight. Then Earthborn took a step back and whipped his arms around his body, still holding Max by the feet. He pulled Max around in a circle, until his body met with the upright of the thick Doric column. Max dropped to the floor, still.

"Shame. I do like dogs", whispered Earthborn. He leant down and recovered his sword. Then he turned. Sir Francis was stood in shock.

"You have killed Maximus", accused Sir Francis.

"So it seems, but for rabid dogs, it's a mercy to put them out of their misery."

"You will regret that, sir. Who are you, and what do you want with me."

"Ah, who I am is a story indeed, but too long to tell now. All you need to know is that the current name is Earthborn, N.W. Earthborn. Or you may know me by another name. Others call me..........VAMPYR HUNTER B!"

"Come again?", replied Sir Francis, perplexed.

"Vampyr Hunter B", said Earthborn, slowly.

"Ah, did you say D?"

"No B."

"Ah!"

"So you have heard of me?" Earthborn said, triumphantly.

"Sorry, no, I am afraid not. I have heard of Vampyr Hunter D. Long dark hair, black hat, black cloak? That is him, is it not?"

"Yes", growled Earthborn.

"Well, he is rather well-regarded, even amongst us night dwellers, despite him being our sworn enemy. It is really hard to dislike him as he had such style and panache. Does he not even have his own range of comic books?"

"Yes", grunted Earthborn.

"And a series of action figures?"

"Yes", snarled Earthborn, "And a film."

"Oh, well I can sympathise with you on that, dear boy. Surely you must have heard of Dracula? That fake Count stole all my stories and made himself-"

"STOP", shouted Earthborn. It was the first time he had spoken above a whisper. "I am not here to discuss the relative merits of who deserves fame. I am here to destroy you."

"Oh. That does seem to put a bit of a downer on this relationship then, does it not?"

"You fool. You have no idea what I have done to you. It was not enough you take your life. First I had to ruin it. Here you are, no friends, no home, no hope. Alone in the.....OUCH!"

It was exactly at that time that Chili bit him on the back of the knee. The green squirrel had taken advantage of two things. Earthborn's soliloquy, and his boot-cut trousers. Chili snuck up his left leg, until he found the tendon at the back of the knee and gnawed through it with his sharp little teeth.

Earthborn lurched to his left side as his leg almost buckled under him. He caught himself by prodding the point of the silver sword in the floor, and used it as a crutch. He shook his leg, painfully, and Chili came flying out, chittering happily. The little squirrel scampered back to Sir Francis, and sat on his shoulder, sticking his tongue out at the already irritated Earthborn.

"You dare?" he whispered in a deadly voice. "Then you shall die as well, away from your precious Flora, as that mutt died without seeing his beloved Henry."

"Wait, how did you know–" enquired Sir Varney.

"Flora and Henry's name? You fool. Do you not see? It was I–"

"That gave me the blood rage, so that I would attack the children? No doubt by placing increasing amounts of blood in my glood? So that the rage grew over time? Then you treated poor Maximus's collar with wolfsbane, so that he would think that Henry was trying to keep him in wolf form. Then over time you stole small precious items and then hid then in Chili's' cage. Then you must have sprayed the cage with something malodorous this very day to prompt Mrs. Bannerworth to ensure Flora cleaned him out and found the loot. No doubt you were also the one that convinced that mortal that extra-terrestrials were living at Ratpole House. No, I had worked all that out thank you. Agatha used to consult with me on her mysteries you know?"

"Oh", was all Earthborn could mutter. He was crestfallen that he could not reveal his plan himself.

"No, the only thing I wanted to ask was how did you know about this place? But I do not suppose that matters now."

"Indeed not, for today you die", whispered Earthborn.

"Is it still daytime? I was convinced it was night."

"That means nothing as this night you will die" Earthborn paused momentarily, and then reluctantly added "Again."

With that, Earthborn launched himself forward, swinging the long silver sword. It whistled through the air in a bright arc. Varney seemed to turn transparent and the sword flew through his incorporeal body without injury.

"You may well have erred there, D. My apologies, B. It does indeed matter. I am strong enough during the day, when rested and out of sight of the sun. But in my mother night, my powers increase tenfold."

With that, Varney solidified and seem to grow taller and wider.

"And also with some blood in my veins, then I can call on my old powers that were, shall we say, altered by the glood. No more emerald rabbits or jade squirrels. And I think I may take the form of my good friend to defeat you. A true child of the night."

The towering figure of Varney started to change. Chili jumped off Sir Francis' shoulder and ran off. The outline glowed and then shrunk lower but became wider. Two legs turned into four, and Sir Francis dropped to the floor on all fours. When the light stopped, a huge wolf stood there. It was easily the size of a pony. It raised its head and howled, and then launched itself at Earthborn.

Teeth and claw fought silver and steel, but neither could lay a blow on the other. For five minutes the fight raged until Earthborn put together a series of strokes that backed the great wolf into a corner. Earthborn smiled, when he saw that Varney had nowhere to go. He raised his sword to strike at the wolf's great chest.

As the sword came down, Varney turned to mist and floated away over Earthborn's head. On the other side of the room, Varney landed and started to solidify into his more usual humanoid form. As quick as a flash, Earthborn spun. His right hand flew to three objects on his belt, and then he cast his arm. Three small darts thudded into Varney's chest, all less than a hands width apart.

Varney staggered back, and plucked the darts from his chest.

"Ha, foolish mortal, they did not hurt me."

"They were not supposed to, foul creature.", and Earthborn once more launched himself forward. Sir Francis changed into mist once more, or at least he tried to. He couldn't. He tried to change into a bat, but again with no effect. He looked down at the darts and saw them gleaming on the floor in the dim light.

"Silver", he grunted.

Then he didn't have time to think, as Earthborn was on him. He managed to dodge the sword, and punched his adversary in the face with staggering power. The blow hardly even caused Earthborn to pause. Varney fought on, striking with blows that would have felled a dozen mortals, but Earthborn seemed implacable, invincible, unstoppable.

Seeing no other option, Varney lunged forward, to sink his fangs into Earthborn's neck. His eyes went deep red in the expectation of blood, as he bit down. Then he felt a cracking, and a sharp pain, and he pulled back. He yowled and reached up his hand to his mouth. One of his fangs had snapped, leaving a sharp stump in his mouth.

Then he felt a hand around his own neck, and he was lifted off the floor, kicking and struggling.

"Fool. You seek to drink the blood of one who has none. You cannot hurt me. I was born to hunt and kill your kind. I was molded into a weapon to destroy all vampires and-"

"Vampyr's", grunted Sir Francis, "Rhymes with-"

But Earthborn just squeezed harder, and Sir Francis could not speak. He hung there, limp like a puppy in its parent's mouth, helpless.

Earthborn raised the huge sword. He pressed a hidden button, and with a click, a pointed ash stake slid out of the pommel of the sword. Now one end it had a long silver blade, the other, a sharp ash stake.

"Hmm, heart or head I wonder. Or maybe both", he whispered, levelling the point of the sword at Sir Francis.

Chapter Twenty Three – Dungeon Crawl

Humans being humans, they tend to be predictable. If they want to storm a house as a mob, they tend to go to the front door, as that's what civilised people do. They break in by the front door, not by sneaking around the back or some other underhanded way. Even mobs have standards.

Ratpole House was doing a fine job of repelling the mob from entering. Tuesday stood in front of the green door, hammering on it with his podgy pink fists. The effect was rather less dramatic that it sounded, as Tuesdays fists soon bruised after a few blows on the hard oak door, and he decided instead to bang the door knocker repeatedly.

"Let us in. let us in" he cried, "We come in peace and only want to welcome you and learn from you."

"The baying crowd do not look especially friendly", thought George as they snuck up the path, keeping in the shadows of the trees and bushes. *"If I was an alien I think I would be trying a different planet to visit."*

But the door was solid, and no matter how much the crowd battered it with hands and feet, it stayed resolute. Some others had got bored and decided to try to force open the window shutters. However a few well-placed splinters soon put them off that idea. Soon, they were just milling around, watching the TV coverage of themselves milling around on their smartphones.

No-one was paying any attention to the children, as they crept through the garden, rather wishing it was still the overgrown jungle they had first encountered. They got to the end of the garden and were around the side of the house, away from the front door. The coast seemed clear, but as the coast was about 80 miles away that really didn't make any difference. However George signaled to Flora and Henry that they would make their way to the bulkhead door into the cellar.

No one in the mob had thought to go around looking for other entrances to the house. There was a good reason for this. Individually, the people in the mob were reasonable, intelligent people. George had spotted Mr. Bopara, the science teacher from his new school (that he was starting next month) in the crowd. From open evenings, he knew Mr. Bopara was a man of science and reason.

However, when a group of people become a mob, then they all of a sudden seem to become stupid, or at least act stupidly. Mobs did not encourage logical thought or reasoning, but more primitive actions, which in this case was good. Therefore the back of the house was empty.

The not so good news was that the bulkhead door was locked solid, seemingly from the inside.

"What do we do now?" Henry asked.

"I am not exactly sure. We need to convince the house that we are friends." suggested George.

"But how do we speak to a house?"

"I have no idea, Flora. I am open to suggestions."

They sat there, backs against the double door, not knowing what to do. Then they heard a clunk from behind the door. They sprang to their feet and moved away, and then saw that one of the doors had opened slightly. George ran forward and pulled it open. A small face appeared behind the door, a green furry face.

"Chili!" shouted Flora.

"Sshhh", warned Henry. It was a secret mission after all and so they all needed to keep radio silence, not that they had any radios with them.

The little squirrel squeaked in delight and scampered over George's head to get to Flora. His little claws caused George to flinch at the stabbing pains, and he nearly dropped the door. Nearly but not quite.

Chili was meanwhile perched on Flora's shoulder, and cheeping and chirping animatedly into her ear.

"From what I can tell, Sir Francis is in trouble. There is a man, a what…?"

Chili chattered away again.

"A bad man, who is trying to hurt Sir Francis."

"And what about Mr. March?" asked Henry, worried.

"He was with Sir Francis and he fought the bad man, but he was… Say again Chili", said Flora, clearly upset by something.

Chili chattered away, but this time in a slower, seemingly sadder tone.

"I'm sorry, Henry, but Chili says he thinks that the bad man killed Mr. March."

The colour drained from Henry's face, and tears started to well in his eyes. He stood still for a few moments.

"Maybe you should go home, Henry, and talk to mum", suggested George, gently.

Henry looked up, anger burning in his blood-shot eyes.

"No, I am going to find this bad man, and if he killed Mr. March, I will kill him", he said savagely.

George just nodded. They opened the door fully, and checked the stairs were there this time (they were) and made their way down into the dark cellar.

Chapter Twenty Four – Heads, Fire or Heart?

There was nothing Sir Francis could do. The hand holding him was too strong, and he could not change form. He had only one chance left. He stared down into the eyes of Earthborn and asserted his will.

"Look at me, look at me", his mind spoke out to Earthborn. *"I demand that you look at me. You cannot resist my will."*

Varney's eyes started to glow hypnotically and he used every ounce of his willpower to drag Earthborn's gaze up to him. He starred deep into the deep brown eyes, projecting his will onto Earthborn. The fingers around his throat started to loosen, and the sword started to dip towards the floor. Slowly, he was working his way into Earthborn's mind, making his will Varney's own.

But then Earthborn just shook his head and laughed.

"Pitiful fool. You seek to overpower my will? But I have no free will. I am commanded by another and so you cannot control me as I have no will of my own."

He started to squeeze again, and the sword came back up.

"Now, every story has its end, and it seems that yours is past due", he smiled.

There are three ways to kill, or kill again, a vampyr. Firstly you can chop their head off and fill the mouth with wild garlic. Secondly you can set fire to them and burn them to death and then scatter the ashes on holy ground. The third is the best known, and that's by putting a stake through their heart (if you can find it. Vampyr's hearts are very small).

"I think my employer will wish to have a souvenir, so heads it is, I think."

He brought the sword back, and then swung it forward towards Sir Francis' thin neck. Sir Francis closed his eyes in resignation.

Chapter Twenty Five – Blood and Flowers

The Bannerworth kids made their way up from the cellar into the main hallway. The green door stood before them, and Tuesday and the most enthusiastic of his mob were still knocking on it.

"First the kitchen", said George, who had his suspicions. They went into the large kitchen and George went straight to the dishwasher. They re-used and re-washed all the glasses used for the glood, and Sir Francis usually put the dishwasher on when he went to bed in the morning. George opened the door, and found what seemed to be the last couple of glasses used. There was a little bit of green residue at the bottom of each, which still hadn't solidified. Glood was quite thick and viscous, and clung to the inside of the glass.

George examined both glasses carefully. At the bottom of each glass he saw something unusual.

"Look at this. Where the glood residue is at the bottom of the glass, there are small specks of red.."

"Red? What do you think it is?" asked Henry

"Blood I would imagine. I think someone's been adding small amounts of blood to Sir Francis' glood, meaning that-"

"He had built up a blood thirst again?", suggested Flora.

"Exactly! Someone has been slowly building him up so that he would fly into a blood rage and try to drink us."

"What about Mr. March?"

"Let's have a look." They walked over to Mr. March's bed. Henry cuddled into it, tears once more forming.

"It still smells of him." He said quietly.

"Where's his collar?" asked George, gently.

"It's normally over there" pointed Henry. George walked over to the windowsill, and the collar was there, resting. It looked sad and lonely without Mr. March. George picked it up carefully and sniffed it.

"There's something odd about it. It smells of…….flowers."

Then he went to the kitchen drawer and found a small, sharp knife. He went back to the collar and unpicked the stitching of the leather. The collar came apart, and in between the two layers of leather was a separate layer of a compressed blue-purple flower.

"That must be the wolfsbane Mr. March was going on about", said Henry.

"Yes, it seems someone tampered with the collar, and stitched this into the lining. I assume it slowly leached into his bloodstream. So at least we know it wasn't you Henry – as you can't stitch straight!"

"Oi!"

"Henry, I am saying it wasn't you."

"Oh, sorry, well of course it wasn't me", cried Henry, upset.

"But now we have proof."

"Not that it matters. Mr. March is gone, and I will never get chance to tell him", said Henry quietly.

George and Flora walked over to comfort him, but as they did Chili raced off towards the parlour. George shrugged and nodded for them to follow. When in the room, Chilli then hared over towards the large fireplace and stood in it, jumping up and down excitedly.

"It seems Chili wants us to go in the fireplace", said Flora, puzzled.

"So it seems" agreed George.

They all walked into the dusty fireplace and looked around, and up, and down.

"What now?" asked Henry.

"Flora?"

"Well, Chili seems to think, if I am understanding correctly, that Sir Francis and Mr. March went this way."

"Hmm, but how?"

"Up the chimney?" suggested Henry.

"Sir Francis, maybe, but I am not so sure about Mr. March. It looks like it gets quite narrow up there" replied George, staring up the chimney.

"Look at this, George", said Henry.

He was pointing down at the floor. On the stone hearth were lines in the dust, semicircular lines that curved around towards the back of the fireplace.

"Well spotted Henry. It looks like something turned around in here. Possibly the fireplace itself. Leading to a-"

"Secret passage!", Henry and Flora exclaimed, excitedly. It was the first time Henry had looked vaguely happy about anything since he heard about Mr. March.

"Yes, maybe so. But how do we open it?"

They searched for secret pedals to press, or secret latches, or stones that moved – but couldn't find anything. Then Flora noticed that the back of the fireplace had been cleaned, or partially cleaned, and there was still the imprint of long, incredibly thin fingers visible in the dust. In the brickwork now visible, there was a narrow hole.

"How about this?" she suggested. Then she reached into her ever present backpack and found a 2B long pencil (or was in not 2B?)*2. She stuck it in the hole, and straight away, there was a rumbling. The whole fireplace started to rotate into the wall.

"Well, here we go", said Henry, as their whole world seemed to turn.

---

2 The author apologises for this terrible joke, but it had to be done

Chapter Twenty Six – Cut Down to Size

Sir Francis braced for the impact of the blade. But then a form jumped from the darkness and latched onto Earthborn's back and sword arm. The weight pulled the arm to the ground, and Earthborn backwards. His grip on Varney loosened and Sir Francis was able to free himself. He dropped back to the ground, not knowing what was happening. What he saw was unexpected to say the least.

A bloody and battered Max was clinging onto Earthborn's back, with one clawed hand clamped around Earthborn's left wrist. He pulled it down, so that the sword was pulled away from Varney.

"Maximus, you faithful wolf. I have rarely been so pleased as to see any creature again", shouted Varney in delight.

Max just grunted, and nodded towards Earthborn.

"Oh, my apologies, you require some aide."

Max nodded frantically.

With that, Sir Francis jumped up and grabbed hold of Earthborn's right wrist. Between the two of them they managed to force Earthborn back. Max swept behind him with his powerful leg, taking Earthborn's feet from under him. The three of them toppled over, but ended up with Earthborn on the ground, with the other two on top of him.

Max concentrated on the sword arm, now using both hands to grab the wrist. He smashed the arm against the hard stone floor again and again, until the sword flew lose from Earthborn's grip, and skittered across the floor. Quick as a flash, Max lept off Earthborn, and bounded across the ground on all fours.

Earthborn grunted and heaved at Sir Francis, who still held his other arm tight. He forced himself to his feet, and the two were locked in combat. Each had one of the other's arms by the wrist and they wrestled. But Earthborn was too strong. He was forcing Sir Francis to his knees, smiling grimly as he did so.

"Fool. You cannot beat me. And now you scramble in the dirt like the parasite you are. You are mine to exterminate…"

"Sir Francis, duck!" shouted Max.

Varney acted, letting go of Earthborn's wrist and going limp. He dropped to the floor and managed to break his wrist free from Earthborn's grip. The tall figure loomed over him.

"…you will be another creature of the night to fall under the blade of Vampyr Hunter…EEEEEEEE-"

"Then you will need your sword" growled a voice behind him.

Then there was a swish, and a surprised look crossed Earthborn's face. He looked down and saw that the silver blade had cut into his torso downwards at an angle, from the left, and the sharp blade cut through his dense body, exiting at the right side, lower down.

"Vampyr hunter E? I thought you were B", queried Sir Francis.

"Well, I never", said Earthborn, as his body slid away from his legs, towards the floor. He lay there in two pieces, blinking in surprise as he stared at his legs next to him. There was no blood, and the two pieces seem to be solid where they had been sliced apart – like if you chopped a piece of clay in half. Max stood there behind Earthborn, and he dropped the long sword to the floor, not wishing to keep hold of it any longer than he had to.

"I think that cut him down to size", he couldn't resist. Varney chuckled,

"That was indeed a mighty stroke, Maximus – I am in your debt. But yes indeed, he is but half the man he used to be", he chortled in return.

"But a most unusual kind of man, Sir Francis. There is no blood, no, erm, other stuff spilling all over the floor. I would expect that if I had chopped a human in half then all over the floor would be org-"

"Enough of that, Maximus. It is indeed strange but it is a mystery for us to ponder later."

"You think it is time to leave, Sir Francis?"

"Yes I do, Maximus. Have you seen Chili?", replied Sir Francis, standing up and brushing himself down. He so hated to get dust and dirt on his black jacket.

"No, Sir Francis, last I saw he was running back up towards the house."

"Ratpole may still not be safe, and we will have to wish Chili our best. But worry not, faithful wolf, I have other safe locations prepared against events like this. Follow me, Maximus!"

With that, the two of them headed away from Ratpole to another exit from the catacombs.

Earthborn lay on the floor, his plan in pieces, as was he. This was embarrassing. He had underestimated the vampyr, and especially his damned wolf. Still, all was not lost. He would simply have to change his target.

He looked over and saw his waist and two legs twitching next to him. They had fallen down so that his feet were by his head. He tried to sit up, but was unable, and then he remembered he didn't have any stomach muscles, or more accurately, his stomach muscles were lying a few yards away at the other end of his feet.

"Hmmm", he thought. He was lying on his back, and he tried to roll his head and torso over, flailing with his arms to generate some momentum. He rolled, and rolled, and then received a foot in his face as his (mainly) disembodied feet kicked him accidentally. He grunted to himself, not in pain, just annoyance. He tried again and managed to flip himself over along his side, so that he was now lying face down in the mud.

He reached up with his hands and found his feet – which was a very weird feeling in itself. His senses struggled to work out where his feet were in relation to the rest of him when he touched them. He ignored his feelings, and started to haul himself up from his feet, up his legs, which kept twitching.

It was slow going as he climbed up his own legs back towards his lower torso. He was very relieved that no one was watching as at times it all looked a bit bizarre as his torso dragged itself up his lower half. After a few minutes, he had dragged himself up past his waist. He lay there and lined up the bottom of his upper body with the lower body and legs. Then he pushed down until the two met.

There was a squelching sound as the two pieces seemed to stick together and started to merge into one. There was just a thin line in the flesh where the sword had cut, but then that started to disappear. He was whole again.

He stood up and dusted himself down, and then promptly fell flat on his face. He cursed and then tried to stand up again. Once more he toppled over. He cursed a few more times. Then he looked down and cursed for a good minute, using some of the swear words he kept for extra-special occasions.

In his hurry to reform himself, he had accidentally managed to put his legs on backwards. And not just his legs. He looked down and saw that his bum was now at the front, his knees bent behind him, and his cowboy boot clad feet were pointing out behind him.

"Confound it" he thought, or something similar to that. Then he reached down, crossing his left hand over to his right hip, and his right hand behind him (although where behind actually was was not immediately apparent) and grabbed his left hip. Then he twisted his arms, and so wrenched around his lower body.

He grunted in discomfort as it was a very odd feeling, but he managed to pull his bum around to the back, and the rest of his legs obligingly followed. He looked down and checked, and he could once more see his pointed toes (the boots were pointed, not his actual toes). He got to his feet again and this time failed to fall over. He patted himself down until he was sure everything was back in the right place. It was, and just in time!

Echoing down the corridor that led back up to Ratpole House, he heard a familiar sound. The fireplace in the parlour was once again being used. He quickly picked up his sword, and melted back into the shadows. Time to invoke Plan B.

Chapter Twenty Seven — Gods and Monsters

They waited for the fireplace to stop turning so they could step out on the other side of the parlour. The only problem is it didn't.

"We are going to have to jump off", cried George, "it clearly spins back around to be back in place for the next person."

They all jumped off the strange merry-go-round. They were in a long, dark corridor. The walls were made up of large stones, and the corridor snaked off in front of them.

The passage was narrow and so they could only walk in single file. There was little light, which wwas a bit of an issue as none of them had supernatural night vision. However they soon solved this, using the torches on their phones as light to navigate by. The passage seemed to be cold and warm, and dry and humid at the same time, and it twisted its way down through the hill-side.

Shortly after that, the descent did indeed level off, and the corridor widened and straightened. Then they emerged into a large antechamber. A combination of Ionic and Doric columns were at each side of the rectangular chamber, supporting the tall roof. The floor was a glorious mosaic of coloured stone and glass.

"Oh look, is that Jupiter?" asked Flora.

"And that must be Neptune", said George.

"And that's mama's favourite, the guy that likes wine", suggested Henry, pointing.

"Yes, Bacchus. We seem to be in an old Roman villa that's been buried over millennia. This is a find of amazing significance. When-"

"-Or if", cut in Henry.

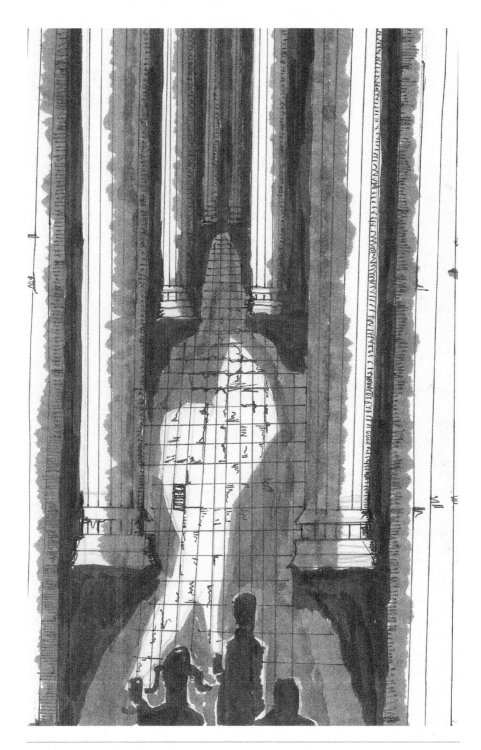

"Thanks Henry", replied George, dryly, "WHEN we get out of this, maybe we will get chance to investigate it."

"But what about Sir Francis", asked Flora.

"And Mr. March!" said Henry, eyes filling up again.

"Yes, sorry, we must concentrate on the matter in hand."

George shone his torch on the floor and saw that there were a lot of footprints in the dust. He could easily make out Sir Francis' footprints, as he liked a pointed shoe with a Cuban heel. There were also some odd hybrid footprints – or paw prints. They seemed halfway between human and animal. The toes were still human shape, but the big toe seemed to be at the back of the foot. Finally, there were some large imprints of what looked like a huge boot – also pointed, but nearly twice the width of Varney's prints.

"There was a massive battle" declared George, "It looked like Sir Francis, and I believe Mr. March, fought a third party. The footprints are huge – They must be about size 14 shoes.

"Over here", shouted Henry.

The other two ran over. Henry was pointing at the floor. Laying there was Mr. March's tweed suit, or most of it. It had been torn, shredded and ripped apart. Henry picked a piece up and placed it against his cheek. He could still smell the rather unusual odour of Mr. March.

"Odd", said Flora, "his ripped jacket, waistcoat and shirt are here, and his shoes, but no trousers. Normally when he changes doesn't he shed all his clothes?"

"Yes", said Henry sadly.

"But there is no blood, or anything" said George, as he finished inspecting the floor. "But here", he said, pointing at the base of a pillar "there's a big disturbance in the dust, as if someone lay here for some time. And here in the centre, there were two long items about 3 foot long lying next to each other."

"And over here, two sets of footsteps" shouted Flora, triumphantly.

"Yes, they are Sir Francis's without a doubt, and he's actually running. He must have forgotten to float."

"How can you tell he's running?"

"All his weight is on the front of his shoes, so you don't get a heel print", George explained.

"And next to him are the human / animal prints. That must be Mr. March – he must still be alive."

Henry grinned.

"Or was then", said Flora.

Henry glowered at her.

"Oops", she said.

"So Mr. March and Sir Francis escaped!", cried Henry in joy.

"Did the other party follow them?" asked Flora.

"No not that I can see, the footsteps stop about here. Which means-"

"It's still in the room", whispered Flora and Henry together.

They all turned around and saw a large shape walk out from the shadows at the back of the room.

George looked at the size of the figure, and said "Oh, cr-!"

Chapter Twenty Eight – Smugglers Retreat

Fortunately it was almost totally dark outside now, which was just as well, as no one could easily see Mr. March. He was still stuck in his Max in-between persona, halfway between man and wolf. He didn't have much time to reflect on the advantages and disadvantages of this form, but there were a few.

For one, he was still able to talk, albeit in a rather gruff accent, as his jaw hadn't elongated to its full extent, and his teeth were still only half their full wolven length. However, they were still long enough to cut his lips and cheek as he did talk – and so he tried not to. He followed along behind Sir Francis, and they made a very strange couple.

Sir Francis was shrouded in black, his long coat almost a cape, the collar turned up to hide his pale blue face. He floated along quickly, just above the pavement, and at quite some speed. Max was no more than a few feet behind him. He had to run to keep up with Varney. When he did run, he was more like a great ape, which was embarrassing to his lupine pride. His arms were considerably longer than usual, almost to match his legs, and he loped along mainly on two feet, but using one arm as a third leg. That he was covered in thick dark fur and was wearing only a ripped pair of tweed trousers would be hard to explain if they were stopped by anyone.

Fortunately the streets were quiet. Everyone was still staring hopefully at the sky outside Ratpole House, hoping to see some foo fighters fly past. So they made good time through the dark streets of Bedlamton.

"Where are we going, Sir Francis?" huffed Max, tasting blood as he lacerated his mouth again. He was concerned that the smell of blood may force Varney into a blood rage, but he didn't seem to have a particular interest in mostly animal blood. Vampyrs can exist on animal blood, but it is seen a bit like the human equivalent of eating food out of rubbish bins, and besides, most vampyrs' are animal lovers.

"Not far, brave Maximus, not far. I have a number of locations around this fair town, and we will soon find safety. Then we can plan our next move."

"Well, that didn't answer my question did it?" thought Max, but he didn't want to appear like a young child continually asking **"Are we there yet?"**

Less than a quarter of an hour later they were in the town centre. They arrived at the main park, that was small and leafy, and at the side of the river that ran through the town. The river was tidal and in years gone by, Bedlamton had been quite an important river port, but those days were gone. The park was surrounded by tall iron railings and Max knew that they locked the gates to the park at dusk, and it was way past then.

"**Over there**", pointed Sir Francis, to the fence. Then he floated up with annoying ease, and glided over the fence. Max grunted, and bent his knees into a crouch, and then jumped. His strong leg muscles propelled him over the fence, clearing it by nearly 2 feet. Then he dropped to the floor noiselessly – well at least he thought he did. To the owls in the trees and the bats flitting around, it was as if a tree had fallen in the forest and someone was there to hear it.

"I feel inclined to warn you that our future accommodation will not be as salubrious and as grandiose as Ratpole House."

Max had never considered Ratpole to be either of those things, or he wouldn't have if he knew what salubrious meant.

They arrived at a small, squat, red brick building not far from the entrance to the park. It looked like it was built in the late Victorian era, and had a rather offensive, acrid odour that surrounded it and permeated the bricks. It was especially harsh on Max's over-developed sense of smell. The metal door was padlocked, but Sir Francis just grabbed hold of it and pulled. There was a groaning and wrenching sound, and then he threw the broken lock to the floor. He opened the door and the full stench hit them.

It was a stink that people, especially boys and men, are far too familiar with. It was a strong stench of ammonia that made Max nearly sick to his stomach, and also gave him the urge to wee everywhere.

"What? Your hideout is the men's public toilet?" he asked, flabbergasted.

"Well, when I bought it in the olden days, it was a bit better kept than this. And besides, there is more to it than meets the eye."

With that, Sir Francis strode in. Max paused for a moment, wishing he had a peg, or a much smaller nose, but then followed. Inside the smell was even worse but Sir Francis didn't seem to notice. Max followed, aware that his feet were bare, and he tried not to think of the contents of the pools of liquid he had to walk through. Sir Francis, or course, just floated over it all.

He reached the far wall, and then he leaned down. In the tiled floor was a hatchway that looked like it hadn't been opened in decades – if not longer. Sir Francis reached inside his jacket and found a large brass key and placed it in the corresponding key hole. It groaned a bit as he turned it but then the hatch popped open slightly. Varney pulled it open and in one smooth movement, and dropped down through the hatch.

Max shrugged, and looked down. The dark hole went down about 20 feet, and he could probably jump down. However there was a ladder bolted to the side of the wall, and he took that down as he didn't know quite what was at the bottom – and he thought he should probably close and lock the hatch as well. His claws made a clack clack clack noise as they caught against the metal rungs, but he was soon down. He was quite surprised by what he saw.

He was in the corner of a large, comfortable room. It had a high ceiling, and was about 20 metres square. There were a few old, wingback chairs, a table, and a kitchen area. There was even a fireplace, with a thin chimney in the wall. There was a door, possibly to other rooms, on one of the walls. Light flooded in via thick opaque glass in the ceiling. In one corner were a pile of old barrels and wooden boxes, at least 100 years old. The room was dusty with lack of use.

"What the?" he asked of Varney, puzzled.

"Ah, you may not know that in days gone by, when the deep river trade was still thriving in Bedlamton, that there was a customs house a bit further down the river. This building was popular with a certain type of entrepreneur who preferred to maximize profit by avoiding pesky things such as taxation."

"Ah, so it was a smugglers bolt?"

"Indeed, Maximus. All sorts of cargo was smuggled into the town via this room: whisky, molasses, saffron, tulip bulbs, gold, wine, ale, lace, salt, tea-"

"Tea?"

"Yes indeed. It was estimated that when this operation was in full flight, in the 1780's, that 60% of tea drunk in England was smuggled in. This building was well hidden and used until the early Victorian times, and then forgotten about and someone built the gentleman's convenience on top of it, using it as a foundation. But there are tunnels under the town where the goods were transported to. There's even a railway line below to transport the heavy goods under the town."

Max plonked himself down into one of the chairs, and was enveloped in a plume of dust. He sneezed once. Happy that he knew what he needed to know about his new accommodation, he turned to a more pressing question. Or questions.

"So who in the blazes was that? Or more to the point, what in the blazes was that?" he demanded of Sir Francis.

"Ah, yes. It would appear that I have become a target of a Vampyr Hunter. Highly trained killers of our kind, they have a Guild based somewhere in Eastern Europe that recruits, trains and equips them. They are ruthless and highly efficient"

"Oh great. So are they some devoted religious organization that are sworn to kill all nosferatu?*" [3]

"Well, they claim to be so, but in reality they are just assassins for hire. But why now after 800 years? I have hardly been a blight on the town since I awoke"

"It is curious, but you have obviously upset someone. So now I know about the who, what about the what? That guy should have been unconscious or even dead from the pummeling we gave him. But he seemed almost impervious to harm – even when I sliced him in half!"

---

[3] *Rhymes with chew, loo, poo

"Indeed, some are mere mortals, others are recruited from damned souls that have met their demise too early in life. The Guild offers them a choice. Death and oblivion, or re-birth into servitude. They become creatures molded and shaped back into human form, but without a soul"

"Molded from what?"

"Not flesh that is for certain", replied Sir Francis, running his tongue over his broken tooth. Then he reached into his mouth and grabbed the jagged shard, and pulled. The tooth popped out, and underneath that was an ivory point showing through the gum line. The tooth had already started to grow back.

"So how do we defeat it, Sir Francis?"

"At the moment, dear Maximus, I really just do not know".

Chapter Twenty Nine – Questions and Half Answers

The shadow walked into the centre of the room. It was a towering man, at least four inches over six feet. He seemed to loom over the children.

"Ah, the Bannerworth clan. Finally, we meet again."

"Again?", asked Flora bravely, "I have never seen you before in my life", she contended.

"No, me neither" said George.

"He looks a bit like the supply teacher we had last half term?", suggested Henry. He rarely forgot a face. His times tables yes, but not a face.

"Oh yeah, Mr..........Stingingbottom?", replied Flora. Despite the tension, they all sniggered at that.

"That's him! Are you Mr. Stingingbottom?" asked George, who hoped not as he had been an awful supply teacher and had given Flora detention. Twice. In the same lesson. But then again, reevaluated George, a poor supply teacher would probably be preferable to some all -powerful agent of the dark. Just about.

"No, I am no feeble "supply teacher". I have traveled here from around the world to stop you-"

"From what?" asked Henry.

"Will you stop interrupting me!?", the Not-Mr-Stingingbottom shouted, "If you let me talk I will tell you sooner, yes?"

"I suppose so", they agreed, staring at their feet. To be fair, he would have made a good supply teacher as it felt like they were getting told off in school – or at least Flora and Henry did. George didn't know as he never got told off.

"I am currently known as Earthborn; Nathaniel Wardost Earthborn-"

The children tried not to giggle.

"Stop it!"

"He's definitely a supply teacher", Henry whispered to Flora, who dramatically failed to keep her face straight as it broke into a rather crooked smile. Earthborn scowled at them but continued.

"And I have been the manufacturer of all your recent misfortunes. Unbeknownst to you, I-"

"Snuck into Ratpole House and infected the glood with human blood, slowly building up the level of blood, so that it gave Sir Francis the blood rage, and so that he would attack us?", said George.

"And at the same time, you sewed wolfsbane into poor Maximus's collar, so that he would think that I was trying to keep him in wolf form", continued Henry. "Which I wasn't", Henry finished proudly, crossing his arms in triumph.

"Yes, Henry. We know. Then you must have kept sneaking into our house, when mummy was at work and we were over here, and stolen small precious items and then hid them in Chili's cage. Then earlier on today you must have dropped a stink bomb or something in the cage to prompt mummy to make me clean him out – and find the missing stuff", Flora carried on.

"And were you also the one that worked with that stupid man outside who thinks Sir Francis is an alien? Is that about right?" summed up George.

"Look, for once would someone please let me explain my own plan?" said Earthborn, obviously irritated. These pesky kids were far too smart for their own good, he thought.

"Is there anything you don't know?" he growled.

"Yes. Two things. How did you get into Ratpole? And why are you doing this?" asked George.

"HA!" said Earthborn, triumphantly. "So you don't know everything."

"No one knows everything", replied Henry "Not even George."

Earthborn scowled again. Scowling seemed to be his favourite facial expression.

"The first is my secret, but I see no harm in answering your second question. I have been employed to kill the vile fiend Varney, and any who associate with him."

"And how's that going?" asked Flora sweetly.

Another scowl.

"He may have evaded me, with the aide of his cowering mutt, but I have another plan. I have exactly what I need to destroy him!"

"Oh, and what's that?" asked George, pretty sure he knew what the answer would be.

"You", growled Earthborn, pointing at them.

Flora groaned, "Oh sh-"

Chapter Thirty – Eighth Wonder

Sir Francis and Max sat despondently in the smugglers bolt. Both were sat on one of the old chairs, opposite each other, but staring into space whilst they tried to work out what to do next. Neither of them had any ideas. Or any good ideas.

"How about we try to set fire to him?" suggested Max.

"Erm, no thank you Maximus. He seems to be comprised of fairly inflammable material, and I myself am not wholly comfortable with fire," Sir Francis replied. "Maybe we could chop his head off?"

"No I don't think so, I chopped him in half with his great sword and it just seemed to inconvenience him. Holy water?"

"How do you expect we get any holy water? Have you forgotten that vampyrs cannot enter hallowed ground unaffected? And you can hardly walk into a church looking like a giant teddy bear."

Max was a bit insulted by this. He may only be half changed, but he definitely looked more lupine than he did ursine.

"OK, bad suggestion, but no need to be mean. How about some sort of exorcism?"

"Do you happen to know a friendly priest that will help a vampyr and a wolf-man to exorcise a creature that may not even be a demon. We can hardly call 0800_EXORCISM can we?"

"Have you got any better suggestions?"

"Silver. Ah, his sword was argentium was it not? How about another precious metal?"

"Which one? And in your long life have you managed to collect a set of platinum daggers or a golden scimitar?"

"No, of course not. Then we are powerless," mused Sir Francis downheartedly.

"So it seems."

They sat there moping for a few minutes, and then bickering like an old married couple, and then moping again. This continued for over an hour.

Just then, in the centre of the room, a golden vortex of light appeared. It started off as a small circle of bright light, but then expanded out until it was about 6 feet in circumference. For a few moments it hung there in the air. Sir Francis and Max exchanged puzzled glances and half rose from their chairs, ready for action.

But then, before they were ready, a small dark outline was seen in the circle. A human shaped outline. It grew bigger as it seemed to walk through the golden light, and then a foot stepped out into the room. A figure followed the foot and emerged from the vortex, which continued to swirl around in the centre of the room.

It was a tall man, dressed in long robes and laden with gold jewelry. He wore an extravagant headdress, which was embedded with diamonds. On his wrists were bracelets of gold, and several intricate golden charms hung around his neck. His face was half covered with a mask, but his eyes were dark and mysterious. His hair was long, dark and curled and fell to his shoulders.

The figure stood still, between Sir Francis and Max, and bowed deeply.

"Hmmmm dmmmd mmds," he said, and then realized he was still wearing his mask. He unhooked it and it fell down to reveal a thin face, with dark brown skin. Each ear had many golden earrings, and his face was clean shaven apart from a thin, immaculately maintained, goatee beard. He smiled, an open friendly smile.

"My most humble apologies. I forgot about the mask. I really do not like this method of transport and the mask helps with the fumes. Considering the space between the worlds is a vacuum, then it's surprisingly malodourous. Why, I do not know. I will have to remember to look into that, when I get time."

Sir Francis and Max glanced at each other, even more puzzled.

"But I digress. Please let me formally present myself. I am Prince Kazim Abdul Al Mohammed, and I am honoured to be the caretaker of the 8th Archive", once again he bowed deeply.

"So you know Mr. H?" asked Max, cautiously.

"Charles, yes indeed. I have known him for many a year, and he is a much valued friend and colleague. I understand he is a friend of yours also?" the Prince asked Max.

"Yes, one of the best", replied Max, who felt a bit underdressed in his torn tweed trousers, compared to the extravagantly attired Prince.

"Who is this Mr. H.?" asked Sir Francis

"Mr. Charles Holland, my friend who owns the bookstore in town." explained Max. Sir Francis hadn't been in the best of ways last time he met Mr.H.

"Ah, that explains everything," replied Sir Francis, still not sure what Max was talking about but he really couldn't be bothered to enquire further.

"Well, I happened to be on my annual visit with Charles. We often travel to each other's Archives to exchange ideas, concepts and books, but mainly for a good gossip. But as I said, I was with him when he happened to notice that you may need aide."

"Really? He got his nose out of a book long enough to see what was happening in the real world?" asked Max, flabbergasted. Mr. H was very able to see what was afoot in the world, when he wasn't distracted by a good book.

"Yes, indeed. Although it may have partly been my fault. I was demonstrating new methods for divining to him, and we happened to overlook your incident in the crypt. Charles was most perturbed and was going to visit you personally-"

Max was shocked. Mr. H very rarely left his shop. The last time he could remember was a certain incident with a certain mad professor.

"-but I persuaded him to let me meet you instead. I have heard much about your wolven form, and was also interested to meet the infamous Sir Francis Varney. Alas, we no longer have nosferatu[4] in my realm, despite our lore stating that they were birthed there in time immemorial"

Sir Francis looked up in interest. Firstly as he quite liked being called infamous, but mainly as no one, not even the elder vampyrs, knew the exact origin of their kind – but it was often debated and subject to various legends and myths.

"Pardon, sir, you claim that vampyr kind were born in your realm. Wherever is this place?"

"If you forgive me, Sir Francis, I feel that the other issue is of greater import. Hopefully, if you get through the night-"

Max did not like the use of the word "If".

[4] Rhymes with agadoo, do, do

"-then we may have time to discuss in detail. I would like nothing more. But this other matter is of great import."

Sir Francis grunted, frustrated, but nodded.

"Excellent. Then we will proceed. Please, attend at the table."

The Prince walked over to the table and reached inside his robes with one hand. He pulled out a thick book, leather bound, and clearly ancient. He placed the book on the table. The front cover read,

"Hubert Wilhelm's Bestiary of Magical Creatures and Beings"

"Please excuse the title. Bestiary seems to be a bit of an insensitive term these days," explained the Prince, "especially as if you turn to V and W you will find references to both your kinds. But the book is very old."

"So, Prince Kazim Abdul Al Mohammed-", started Max.

"Ah please, my friend, Kazim is more than acceptable."

"Thank you. Kazim, so Mr. H sent you with this book?"

"Indeed, and he marked the page that you should pay premium attention to."

Sir Francis reached down with his extraordinarily long fingers and opened the book to where a book-mark (from the gift shop at Whitby Abbey) was placed. It opened at "G"

"A "gogmagog?"", asked Max "what in the blazes is one of them?"

"Ah, no. that is a distorted human body twice the normal size. It is the entry after this, and before "gremlins"," replied Kazim.

"Oh. A golem", said Sir Francis.

"A what?"

"It is a figure molded into a human form, made from earth and clay. Often it is a re-birth of one who has died before their time, but when reincarnated as a golem, they lack a human soul and are given a new name" explained Kazim.

"So, it's a dead person in a clay body?" summarised Max, fairly crudely.

"Yes indeed, just so", replied Kazim, smiling.

"And are they hard to destroy?"

"Alas, they are formidable and difficult to stop. But there are methods. If you read on, you will be illuminated."

"Clay.....blah blah blah.....very strong...blah blah blah....immune to most injuries......blah blah blah. Yes we know all this, as we found out ourselves. Get on with it man. Ah, here we go. Iron! There we are, Maximus, I told you it would be a metal", crowed Sir Francis delightedly.

"Precious metal, you said," corrected Max.

"Well it's all relative," retorted Sir Francis, not to be denied his small victory, "If you lived in the bronze age, then iron would be very precious."

Max gave up. **"So how do we kill it?"**

"Iron spikes. We need to embed seven iron spikes in the body, so that it forms a crucifix. Oh, why is it always a crucifix? It is so unimaginative. It would be nice if it was a circle, or a pentagon for a change", complained Varney. He had an irrational dislike of crucifixes, which was completely rational.

"**Well that doesn't sound too bad. as long as we can find some iron spikes**", replied Max.

"Read on, Sir Francis", suggested Kazim.

"Blah, blah blah, form of a cross, blah blah, one in each limb, three in the body, blah blah blah. Oh . . . .", Sir Francis stopped dead, which he would as he is dead, and looked worried.

"**What**?" asked Max.

"The final spike should be placed in the heart of the creature, but it needs to be inscribed with its name."

"**Well, we know that,**" said Max confidently "**it's Earthborn. Nathaniel Wardolf Earthborn, I think,**" he finished, not quite so sure.

"No, its true name. As Kazim said earlier, Earthborn is not his original name. He was re-christened when he was re-born. And we need to find it."

"**But how? That's impossible isn't it?**"

"Maybe not, master wolf, if you read on," Kazim interjected.

"**The name assumed by the golem must be linked to the original name of the subject.**" read Max, leaning over Sir Francis' shoulder. Sir Francis was a bit annoyed by this. He wanted to read out the solution.

"So the clue to his true name is in his current name? "suggested Sir Francis.

"Just so, my lord," confirmed Kazim. "But it is with that, I must leave you. The vortex is starting to fade. I wish you well in your endeavors this night, my friends. If you triumph-"

"Another "IF"" thought Max "that's hardly reassuring"

"-Then I look forward to us reacquainting at Charles' home, when you return the book."

Kazim bowed once more, and then turned and walked into the swirling vortex. Then it winked out of existence.

Chapter Thirty One – King of the Castle

"You understand?" demanded Earthborn.

George and Flora nodded.

"Good, no mistakes, or else young Henry here will suffer for it", he continued. "I would prefer not to harm you directly, but will do it if needs be. Understand, in this I have no choice."

Earthborn stood with his large hand around the back of Henry's neck.

"We will leave and make our way through the streets. You two will go in front, and I will follow with Henry. If you make any noise, or attract any attention, or try to escape, then I will snap young Henry's neck, as if it were a twig. Understand?"

"Yes, we understand!" shouted George in anger.

"But before we go, where is that green rat that follows you everywhere?"

"He is not a rat, he's a squirrel, and he's called Chili", cried Flora in annoyance.

"I care not what he is. But I need him, as I have a task for him."

"You won't hurt him?"

"No no, I need him alive. For now at least", he smiled, unpleasantly.

Flora, unsure, called and Chili raced up from where he was hiding, and climbed up to Flora's shoulder. Earthborn reached inside his voluminous coat, and withdrew a piece of folded vellum paper, and some string.

"Girl, take this and secure it to the animal, so that it will not come loose."

Flora did as he asked, managing to tie the note around Chili's neck with the string.

"Listen, creature. You will need to find the vampyr. You will need to give him this note. If you cannot, or do not, find him, then know that when the clock strikes the twelfth time at the witching hour, then it will bring the doom of the children." said Earthborn. "Your only hope if saving them is to get this message to the vampyr. Does he understand?" Earthborn asked of Flora.

"Of course he does, he was, or is, a professor you know," replied Flora, offended. Then she whispered to Chili, "You do understand don't you?"

Chili stared back at her solemnly and nodded. "Then go", said Flora sadly. Chili circled around the ground until he picked up the scent of Sir Francis and Max. Varney had a feint scent of dust and dried blood, whereas Max had a much stronger odour of wet dog. When Chili caught the scent, he scampered off without another squeak.

"Excellent, Flora. You had best hope that your furry friend can fulfil his task. But now we leave". Earthborn picked up his trunk with one hand, and kept the other around Henry's neck.

They headed towards the exit that Varney and Max had fled through not so long ago. Outside the streets were dark and quiet. The moon was high and lit the cobbled streets with a silvery glow.

"Where are we heading, Nathaniel?" asked George. He tried using the hulking figure's first name to build up a rapport. He had read that when taken hostage, you had to try to build up a relationship with the hostage-taker.

Earthborn just smiled thinly at him, fully aware of what George was trying to do, but appreciating his attempt. He could not underestimate this child, he reminded himself, as he should have realised.

"You will find out. We will play a game, whereby I will tell you when to turn, and you will do it."

"A bit like "Simon Says"?" asked Henry nervously. He didn't appreciate being the hostage, just because he was the smallest.

"If you like, as long as you obey my orders."

They walked into the town centre, down by the river, which split the town in two. There was an old humpback bridge that was the main route over the river, and Earthborn told them to head for that.

"Hmm, we seem to be heading towards the oldest part of town," thought George, trying to figure out their destination.

The current town of Bedlamton was at least a thousand years old. Over the bridge was the original part of the town, with the original town hall, a small quayside and church. There was even a motte-and-bailey castle at the top of the hill, looming over the town.

They walked down to the bridge and went across.

"Turn right", said Earthborn.

"So we are heading to the castle?" said George.

"You will soon see, young master," Earthborn replied.

The path led them out of town, and up the hill towards (as George had guessed) the old castle. It was dark and foreboding against the night skyline. The castle had fallen into disrepair, and had received little attention from the local council. They walked up towards it, and an iron gate secured the main entrance. Earthborn put down his bag, and grabbed hold of the gate with one hand – as his other was still around Henry's neck - and wrenched. It squealed in protest as it was pulled from its hinges. Earthborn threw it to one side, where it landed with a clang against the wall.

"Through here", he grunted.

They walked into the inner square and Earthborn pushed them to the stone stairs that led up towards the battlements. They climbed up the steps and Earthborn pushed them though a dark doorway at the top. They found themselves in a vaulted room that must have been the chapel of the castle.

In the room there were still some old oak benches and Earthborn placed Henry on one, and signaled Flora to sit next to him.

"Stay there," he instructed them both. He turned to George.

"Come over here. We must talk" said Earthborn quietly and walked off to the other side of the room. George looked up and shrugged and followed. He sat down next to the large man, who had seated himself on another wooden settle.

"Your mother never really told you what happened to your father, did she?"

"Yes, she did, he died when he was abroad for work. Car accident," replied George, sadly.

"A car accident. Yes, well from a certain perspective that may be true. You were old enough to remember? I doubt Flora and Henry remember much."

Henry was just a toddler when his dad died, and Flora was only three and had just vague images of him. But George remembered everything about that terrible evening.

"Yes I do remember but why do you care? I don't want to talk about my family history with such a villain."

"A villain, well, yes I suppose I am, by deed if not by thought," Earthborn replied. He looked almost sad.

"However, your mother may not know everything about your father's death," he carried on.

"What do you mean?"

"Can you not see, George?" Earthborn continued, removing his hat for the first time, and leaning down towards George. Brown eyes stared at George from beneath his shaggy white-blonde hair, which was slightly unruly.

George stared back, his own brown eyes looking unbelievably at Earthborn.

"Yes, you can see it can't you?" the eyes staring back were almost identical to his. The hair was almost the exact colour as Henrys, and the mouth mirrored Flora, when she was in a mood.

"Yes, I am your father", whispered Earthborn, "Or was."

Chapter Thirty Two – High Stakes

"**Well,**" said Max "**that was unexpected.**"

"Indeed, but most useful," replied Sir Francis "at least we know the nature of the beast that we face."

"**Yes, but not where he is or how to find him.**"

"True, Maximus, but one step at a time. First, let us devise a plan to defeat this creature. I fear if we do not find him, that he will find us. He seems most determined."

"**So we know we need some iron stakes-**"

"Please, use another word, Maximus. That word I like not, for obvious reasons."

"**-Iron spikes,**" corrected Max, barely missing a beat. Sir Francis nodded in approval. "**Where are we likely to get any of those at this time of night?**"

"Is there nowhere in the township?"

"**Well there's the ironmongers on Zetland Street; the forge near the old castle; and the iron wholesalers at the retail park. But they will all be closed now.**"

"Blast it, Maximus, then how do we progress? I do not want to wait the evening outwith this fiend on our tail. He may find me as I sleep in the morn. This needs to end, TONIGHT!" Sir Francis emphasized this by slamming his clenched fist on the table, which he accidentally broke in two.

"**I agree, Sir Francis, but let's not lose our noggins, but use them instead.**" Max replied, trying to calm the agitated vampyr. "**Did you say there was a railway here? Is it still intact?**"

"Yes and yes, but why?"

"Well, don't the railways use iron stak........sorry.....spikes to nail down the railway lines?"

"Why, yes, I think they may have. Capital thinking Maximus. Follow me."

Sir Francis leapt up from his chair, or more floated up aggressively, and drifted towards the other doorway from the room. Max followed as instructed, his nails clacking on the hard stone floor.

At the end of a short corridor there was a wooden hatch in the floor, which Sir Francis wrenched open, and without hesitation, floated down. Max once again took the safer approach and used the metal ladder bolted to the wall. Once again he descended into darkness.

At the bottom, there was a tunnel ahead of them. It was low, and arched and made of old brick. Running through it was a narrow gauge railway line, the type used in mines for hand-carts rather than for steam trains. On the line were three old carts, made of wood and iron. Max jumped onto the line, and tried to move a cart out of curiosity. It was stuck solid, and when he looked down he saw that the brakes had rusted onto the thin metal wheels. He shrugged, and turned his attention to the metal lines.

Short wooden boards ran underneath the double line of rails, that went underneath the rails, and from side to side every three feet or so. Inspecting closely, Max saw that they were secured to the boards by inch thick iron spikes that had been hammered into the wood. They had a flattened hooked end, so they could be prized out and replaced.

Max looked around and saw an old pick-axe leaning against the wall, doing nothing. He picked it up and shook off the dust. It enveloped him and he sneezed several times as it went up his extremely sensitive nose. Werewolves were well known for having allergies. He placed both hands on the thick yew handle, and flexed it to see if the wood was rotten. It was still firm and springy.

He placed the end under the first spike he came to, and pulled the handle back. The spike groaned in protest as time had almost welded it in place, but eventually gave under Max's prestigious strength. It popped out of its hole, and Max reached down and picked it up.

The spike was black and rough, and about six inches long with a point about an inch long at the end. Max flipped it over, so that he was holding it with the point towards him, and the length of the spike was rested diagonally across his palm. He closed his hand around it, and turned and bent his arm over his shoulder. Then he straightened his arm forward, and the wrist gave a slight flick at the end.

The spike flew from his hand, and turned end over end. Then it thudded, point first, into a wooden board that was leaning against the wall. It quivered as it was buried halfway in the wood. Max grunted in approval.

"Excellent shot, Maximus, truly excellent."

"Thank you Sir Francis, helps that I worked in a circus when I was younger," Max replied. Then without further ado, he prized more spikes out, until they had a baker's dozen.

"Best to have spares," explained Max. Sir Francis nodded in agreement. Max looked around and found an old leather shoulder bag on a peg, and slung it over his head. He placed the spikes inside. They climbed, or at least Max did, back up the ladder and returned back to the main room.

"**Now all we need to know is where he is, and his true name**", sighed Max.

"Here's hoping something will present itself, Maximus."

"**Yes, Sir Francis, but it's not like this is a TV show, where things just happen in the nick of time.**"

Then, just in the nick of time, a small, creature dropped into the room. It landed in the bottom of the fireplace with a puff of coal dust. It was covered in soot, and had a long bushy tail.

Varney hissed and took a step back, bearing his fangs (one and a half of them) and raising his hands like claws before him. Max dropped to all fours, his fur on its end, and snarled.

The filthy creature chittered excitedly, and Max cried "**It's Chili!**"

Chili shook himself and some of the soot dislodged from his fur, so he was now a mucky green. Then he chattered once more. This time the tone was more irritated.

"**There's no need for language like that Chili, we weren't to know**", said Max gently.

Chili ran over to him and ran up his leg and body, up to Max's shoulder where he perched himself. Max sneezed once more from the dust, causing Chili to dig his claws in with fear. Max cried out in pain.

"**Ouch, you little........but you say you were sent by the big mean man?**"

Chili nodded pointed at his neck. Tied around it was a parchment. Max untied in, and unfolded it. It was also very dusty, but the inside had been kept clean. He skim read it, his mouth moving as he read, commenting "oh my", "Oh dear" and various, more fruity terms as he read it. When he had finished, he frowned and walked over to Sir Francis, saying,

"I think you need to read this". Sir Francis took the vellum parchment and started to read, **"and try not to get too angry."**

To Sir Francis Varney
Once of Ratpole House
Currently of No Fixed Abode

My dear Sir Francis,

I had hoped you would make this easy and not involve others. However, it seems that, as I should have expected, you are nothing more than cowardly vermin. You will, it seems, use and sacrifice your friends in order to save your worthless skin.

If you think that is an unfair assessment, then I give you a chance to disprove it. By fleeing, you have forced my arm. I have had to involve others that I would much rather not harm – but I will do if I am forced.

I have with me three children, who I am assume you are well acquainted with. They are most exceptional children. Brave, resourceful and loyal, qualities that you yourself are sadly missing.

If you have any regard for these youngsters, then you will be at the old castle, by the time that the church clock rings the last of the witching hour. Failure to do so would be, shall we say, unfortunate for the children.

By all means bring your pet dog. I am prepared for him now, and fear not a mangy mutt. I only hope that he is house trained as I would not like to see him fouling the floors of the ancient castle.

Yours (un)faithfully,

Nathaniel Wardost Earthborn.
A.K.A Vampyr Hunter B.

"Wardost, I was close", said Max to himself.

Varney snarled and crumpled up the letter and threw it to the other side of the room.

"What hour is it Maximus?"

"About half an hour before the witching hour"

"Then we had best make haste. I will prove to this creature of mud that I am faithful and loyal to my friends. And if he harms one hair on their heads...." he stopped himself.

"But why the castle?" he mused "surely he would have been better choosing hallowed ground?"

"Such as the church?"

"Yes indeed. As I am sure you are aware, we night walkers have difficulty with holy ground. It robs us of much of our vitality and strength. But he chooses the battlefield, but not to his advantage. That is most concerning."

"Or good for us" suggested Max, trying to be more upbeat. Sir Francis stayed silent, but there was something in the corner of his mind that was bothering him.

"Well, before this night is done, we will discover our fate. Let us go, with utmost haste."

With that, they headed towards the exit. Soon they were on the streets of Bedlamton, heading towards the old part of the town. They were only a few minutes into their journey when all of a sudden Varney staggered and almost fell to the ground. Then he stood there, swaying and looking confused.

"Sir Francis, what is it?"

"It has been too long since I have eaten anything. The blood Earthborn forced me to imbibe is used up, and I have no glood to sustain me. I fear I will be of little use in the coming battle."

Varney steadied himself, a determined look on his face. He would defend the children, even if it did cost him his (un)life.

"Nonsense. You make your way to the castle, Sir Francis, and I will meet you there," and with that Max sprinted off.

Varney continued on weak legs to make his way to the castle.

Chapter Thirty Three —We are Family?

"My father? You? Oh come off it, have you been watching too many space operas? And I suppose I have a twin sister who happens to be a princess somewhere as well do I? And I have always wanted my own laser sword," said George, more than a bit sarcastically.

"Sometimes truth is stranger than fiction, George," Earthborn's face had softened, and no longer scowled. His eyes seemed to widen and grow warmer.

"Mmm, one thing is true, this is indeed strange."

"But cannot you see it George? Look at me, cannot you see the likeness?"

"No I can't. You don't look like us," George lied "and you've just kidnapped us and threatened to snap Henrys neck. Not a very fatherly act is it?"

"But there were circumstances. I had no choice."

"Everyone has a choice."

"I don't. I am compelled to do as I am instructed. And-"

"Who by? Who instructs you?"

"That is a long story George, and I fear you are not ready for it yet. One thing you must know. I did die that night six years ago, but as my soul left my body I was given a choice. A choice to be re-born as something other than human, but the price was that I had to obey those that brought me back."

"So you are not human? Is that what you are saying?"

"It may be easier if you saw for yourself," said Earthborn. He removed his coat and started to unbutton his rawhide waistcoat.

"Erm, steady on. Mother has warned us about people like you. What are you doing?" said George, backing away.

"You shall see," said Earthborn. His vest now undone and discarded, he unbuttoned his blue linen shirt, and then slipped it off his shoulders.

George gasped. Earthborn's torso was broad and lean, and well-muscled, but George hardly noticed that. What he saw was that Earthborn's skin was a glistening, smooth brown substance, and cut into it were various tattoos that looked like glyphs and sigils. The lines of the markings seemed to glow slightly, in an ethereal green.

George's fascination was so great it overcame his fear. He walked over and raised his hand, and prodded Earthborn in the ribs with one finger. The tip of his finger made an indentation in Earthborn's skin, and soon his finger was up to its first knuckle, pressing into Earthborn's body. It was like sticking your finger into warm modelling clay.

George pulled it back, and saw the indentation immediately seal itself. The skin was once again clear and unmarked – from the finger prod anyway. Earthborn re-buttoned his shirt up.

"But…" started George, who suddenly found he was lost for words (a very rare occurrence).

"I was re-born as a thing of clay and mud, earth and dirt. I still remember all that I was, but I am cursed as they have not returned my soul – and so I must obey them. I have no power of free will."

"But you have been trying to kill us", George accused.

"Not so!" protested Earthborn. "My orders were to kill Varney and any that associated with them. When I realised that you, my children, were associating with him, then I did all I could."

"And what could you do?"

"I reasoned that if I was able to stop you associating with the vampyr, then I could avoid having to harm you."

"So you used a loophole?"

"I suppose so. Nothing can stop me from killing the vampyr, and his dog, but now you are no longer his friends, you are safe from me. It was all I could do."

"But you threatened us", shouted George.

"Pure bluff and bluster, George. My original plan did not work, as I had not counted on the dog-"

"Werewolf!"

"-Werewolf being such a loyal friend and fierce opponent. If I had been able to dispatch Varney then, there would have been no need for this unpleasantness."

Earthborn knelt down, so that his face was level with George's. He placed a hand on each of George's shoulders, and looked deep into his eyes.

"I only came back as I could not face eternity without being there to see you, Flora and little Henry growing up. I have tried to work my way back to England, and find you, but my masters have kept me busy elsewhere. Ironically, this time, they did not realise that they were sending me to you."

"Is it really true? Can it be you, father?" George asked tearfully. He was starting to believe.

Earthborn pulled George to him and hugged him fiercely. George buried his head into Earthborn's shoulder and realised it was all true. This really was his fath-

"PUT HIM DOWN YOU FIEND, OR YOU WILL FACE MY WRATH," creamed an unearthly voice from behind them.

Earthborn and the children turned towards it. Framed in the doorway was Sir Francis, his face pale blue, his eyes glowing red with anger. The children had never seen him looking so furious.

Earthborn stood up and glared at Varney. His eyes, which moments ago had been soft and compassionate, grew cold. His mouth curled into a snarl of hatred.

"Vampyr", he said quietly "you are mine now."

George clung to him, pleading "Father, if it is you, you do not need to do this. Sir Francis is my friend. Please do not harm him."

Earthborn pushed George away, and said "I am sorry, my son, in this I have no choice," and he walked over and picked up his sword that was leaning against the settle. He held it in front of his face, in a formal salute to his enemy. And then he launched himself at Varney.

Chapter Thirty Four - Withdrawls

Max ran though the near deserted streets at full pelt, or as fast as he could on two legs. His arms were not quite long enough for him to run smoothly on four legs, and it may look a bit odd if customers leaving the pub saw a furry man running though the town centre like a dog.

He made his way quickly and directly as he knew exactly where he was going, as he used to work there as a porter. He ran up the driveway to the large complex, which seemed to be comprised of lots of interconnected box like buildings. There were signs everywhere, pointing to different departments, but he did not need them. There was security at all the main entrances, and he no longer had his pass card, but he knew other ways in.

Open staff entrances were always easy to find, as a lot of the complex was still powered by steam. Even on the coldest nights, the lower corridors was as hot as a sauna. He soon found a doorway propped open by a chair, on which an overflowing ashtray was placed.

He slipped through the doorway into the brightly lit corridor. He used all his senses, and couldn't hear or smell another human within 100 yards of him. But he was still aware that he was just clad in a pair of shredded trousers.

He crept down the maze of corridors until he found a room saying "Staff changing". He listened and sniffed, until he was happy that it was mid-shift and there was no one in there. He pulled the door open a crack and slipped through the gap. He was in the men's locker room. He looked around and saw hanging on the wall a long white coat. He grabbed it, and pulled it on.

Despite being large and volumous for a human, it only just stretched over his abnormally broad shoulders. He managed to button it up, although it gaped in places. He looked around for shoes but there were none that would fit on his large, paw like feet. Instead he found some slip on plastic shoe covers, the kind used by crime scene investigators, and managed to pull them on. He managed to only pierce them with his claws in two places.

He walked quickly down the corridors, turning left here, right there, until he found the room he was looking for. It was lit with bright fluorescent strip lights, and each wall had rows and rows of tall fridges with clear glass doors. He walked along examining them. The fridges had labels on the front saying A, B etc.

He found the one he was looking for. The fridge had a lock on the door, but he pulled at it, and it gave easily, with a snap. Inside were hanging rows and rows of plastic pouches. He grabbed three, and slammed the door closed. Then he made his way to the exit as quickly as he could.

As he left, he pulled off the coat and kicked off the plastic shoes. The bell in the church tower started to ring. One chime. It was nearly midnight.

Holding his precious cargo firmly, but being careful of his claws, he ran off towards the castle. The clock rang 5.

Chapter Thirty Five – Blood and Earth

The clock rang 11. The sword swung down. Varney dodged backwards through the doorway as the blade arced through the air. It hit the door frame, and sparks flew when it made contact with the hard stone.

He backed away into the corridor, feeling weak. He was alone against Earthborn. In his pocket he had half a dozen of the iron spikes, but he didn't trust his aim in his weakened state. He expected Earthborn to follow him and attack him again, but instead he held back, moving to the centre of the room.

"You do not seem yourself this evening, vampyr. Are you feeling a bit under the weather? It would be such a shame, as I would much rather defeat an enemy at the height of their powers. Where is the sport in simply putting a sick animal down, eh?" Earthborn laughed.

Sir Francis was tempted to cross into the room, but felt there was something wrong.

"Come now, vampyr, it is just you and I. Enter and we will fight to the end, and see who is truly the strongest", taunted Earthborn.

Varney went to walk through the doorway, but George shouted,

"No, Sir Francis its hall-"

Earthborn spun and roared at George to be quiet, drowning out the rest of warning. Gone was the compassion and care in Earthborn's eyes. They were now cold and distant. A killers eyes.

"Come, nosferatu[5], let us fight as our forebears have done for millennia. Vampyr against hunter. Surely you would relish the combat?"

---

[5] Rhymes with "whatever will Varney do?"

Sir Francis once more backed away. Earthborn paced up and down in the vaulted room, his eyes never leaving Varney's face.

"A pity, you show yourself to be a coward, as I suspected. If you will not come to me, then I must come to you."

Earthborn ducked as he went through the low doorway into the corridor, and swung at Varney, who dodged back. He fell, weakened, and toppled down several steps in the spiral staircase. Earthborn leapt down, swinging the sword again, and Varney only just managed to duck under it. Fortunately the length of the sword made it hard for Earthborn to swing it effectively in the narrow stairwell.

Next, Earthborn lunged, the tip of the sword aimed at Varney's thin torso. Sir Francis flung himself to one side, and again tumbled further down the steps. He clambered to his feet.

Earthborn closed in on him, his sword pointed at the vampyr's heart. Varney cowered back, powerless, realising that he hardly had the strength to dodge once more.

Earthborn smiled thinly, and then thrust with the sword. As he did, a voice shouted **"Sir Francis, catch!"**

Then a clear plastic pouch filled with a dark liquid flew up the centre of the stairwell. Max's powerful throw was accurate, and Sir Francis used the last of his strength to jump over the stairwell, just as Earthborn's sword struck the wall exactly where Varney had stood a split second before.

Varney fell, but as he did he caught the pouch. He ripped it open with his sharp fingernails, and drank deeply. The red liquid flowed down his throat and permeated his body.

"Hmm, AB+" he thought "Maximus has not forgotten my favourite, it seems".

207

The litre was gone before he even reached the ground twenty feet below. When he did, he landed lightly, next to Max. The wolfman handed him two more pouches, and Sir Francis devoured them with enthusiasm.

"Special occasion, Sir Francis. This time only, OK?" asked Max, nervously. Sir Francis just smiled, a blood red smile. He seemed to grow taller, his thin face filled out slightly, and his eyes glowed red with fury and vigour. He floated up the centre of the stairwell, power emanating from him.

Earthborn stared down in horror and dodged back as the vampyr rose in all his power. He floated in the air above the tall man, who swung his sword. Varney simply dissipated into mist, and the sword passed through him. Then he solidified and struck, his palm striking Earthborn in the chest and knocking him back a few feet.

"Finally, that silver has left my body," Varney thought to himself.

Earthborn kept trying to strike, but was unable to lay a blow on Varney, who struck him in return again and again. The tall figure, terrified, scuttled up the stairs and back into the arched room. Varney floated up effortlessly.

Earthborn ran back and picked up Henry in his spare hand and placed the edge of his sword against the young boy's throat.

"If you want him, you leach, you will have to come and get him", screamed Earthborn.

Sir Francis floated towards the doorway.

"No" screamed Flora and George as one, "Stay out it's-", but Earthborn screamed at them, once more drowning out any warning.

Sir Francis floated through the doorway, and unknowingly into the castle's abbey.

Chapter Thirty Six – Fangs and Claws

The clock struck 12. Sir Francis floated into the room, and hung in the air, radiating power. He looked down at Earthborn.

"Here I am, man of mud. If you want me, come and get me," he smiled horrifically.

Earthborn looked up and smiled and then said, "But of course, I have no wish to harm children." And he released Henry, who ran over to George and Flora. "However, you have misstepped. You do not realise where you are?"

"In an old room in an old castle, of course", replied Varney, puzzled by this enquiry.

"Not just any room, this is the abbey, where the monks said mass a thousand years ago. You have strayed onto hallowed ground, my lord," he finished, mockingly. He pointed up at a wooden cross on the wall.

"Eh," said Sir Francis, "surely not. I cannot feel anyth-"

Then he shuddered in midair. He started to fall to the ground, and struggled to maintain his descent. He tumbled to the ground and lay there in a heap, disorientated.

"Ha, look at you, weak before me. Now your life, or your death, is mine to take." Before advancing, Earthborn reached up and pulled the wooden crucifix from the wall and advanced on Varney.

Sir Francis scuttled back, seemingly terrified, as Earthborn advanced. He stalked the vampyr, sword in one hand, crucifix in the other. Soon Sir Francis found himself backed into a corner, on the ground, groveling before the cross.

"I have you now," said Earthborn, and he pushed the cross even closer to Varney, so that it was about to touch his face. Varney threw up his arms, helplessly, to ward off the one symbol that had power over him.

Earthborn pulled back his arm to strike with the sword. He smiled thinly.

But then Varney's hand shot forward with supernatural speed. It caught Earthborn's sword hand, pushing it back. Then the vampyr's other hand grabbed the cross, grinning. He rose to his feet and pushed Earthborn back seemingly effortlessly.

"But how?"

"Ah, you forget your lore", mused Varney, almost sadly. With that the crucifix went up in flames, a deep blue-purple flame that was in no way natural. The flames engulfed both Varney and Earthborn's hands. The vampyr smiled, whilst Earthborn screamed. The cross burnt with unholy fire and soon was nothing but cinders.

Earthborn finally managed to pull his burnt hand back. It smelt of scorched earth. He dropped his sword and nursed his stricken arm with the other.

"But I don't understand?"

"No, I supposed not. Maybe I should explain," replied Sir Francis, "but maybe not", he smiled. His hand darted to his pocket and he pulled out two iron spikes. He flung one. It pierced Earthborn's left shoulder. Then he hurled the second, and it stuck into Earthborn's right shoulder.

"Two", counted Varney under his non-existent breath.

Then Max was next to him. He also threw two spikes, and they thudded into Earthborn's torso. The large man staggered back.

"**Four**", replied Max, smiling grimly.

Then they both raised their arms and cast them. Two more spikes flew through the air into Earthborn's torso.

"Si**X**", Varney and Max said in unison.

"**Now what?**" asked Max?

"Hmm, yes, to be honest I did not think we would get this far" admitted Sir Francis.

Meanwhile, Earthborn stood there, looking down at the stakes embedded in him. He pulled at the ends, but they were stuck, snagged in his clay like flesh. He shrugged. They caused him no pain, and unless they knew his true name then they would cause no harm.

He walked over to his trunk and threw the lid open. In it was a wrist mounted crossbow, which he strapped onto his useless right hand. It was activated by the nerves in the wrist, and so did not need his shriveled fingers. He loaded it with a cartridge of self-loading, fire hardened, ash bolts. Then he picked up his sword with his left hand. This time they would die, both of them.

Sir Francis and Max spread out, watching as Earthborn approached. He did not seem weakened by the spikes, but seemed even more determined. He raised his sword and pointed, and bellowing,

"Prepare to meet your doom, vermin."

"**Sir Francis, I will keep him busy. You go to the children, they may know his name.**"

"It is worth a try, Maximus. Fight well."

Max turned and stared at Earthborn, who was fast closing the distance. With a howl he darted forward and jumped at the tall figure. He managed to get his feet on Eartborn's bare chest, and the claws of his hands wrapped around each of his wrists. He scratched frantically with his feet, but just dug out divots of earth. Earthborn pushed back, forcing Max back to the ground. He tried to fight back, but Earthborn was too strong. He forced Max's hands back, bending them painfully.

Max howled once more, half in rage, half in agony, and then felt something change. His hands started to grow, as did his arms. His nose elongated, until it was a long muzzle, filled with razor sharp canines. His ragged trousers finally split, as his haunches grew thicker and more powerful and a thick tail forced its way out of the base of his spine. His amber eyes grew rounder, and his ears moved up his head into points on the top of his skull. He grew a good two foot in height, but was now almost twice his normal weight – all muscle, bone and tendon. All fangs, fury and claws.

The great wolf Maximus raised his head and howled in triumph, forcing Earthborn to stagger backwards under the new onslaught. The two behemoths fought, hand to hand, slamming each other into walls with a power that shook the room.

Meanwhile, Sir Francis raced over to the children, who were hiding in a corner, behind an upturned settle.

"George, Flora, Henry. Please forgive me. I–"

"Yes we know," said Flora quickly

"We worked it out," said Henry, rather smugly

"It was all Earthborn," continued George.

"Then no more time to waste. He has a weakness. To destroy his body, we need to pierce him with seven iron spikes. Maximus and I have managed six–"

"-So what's the problem?" asked Flora, "Just stick him with the last one", she continued fiercely.

"Ah, but therein lies the conundrum, dear girl. The last spike must have his true appellation on it"

"Apple what?" said Flora

"Apologies, name, his name"

"Easy", said Henry "it's Nathaniel Wardrobe Earthborn"

"Wardost, I think Henry"

"Very good, it is, but that is not his true name. We must use the true name he had when he was turned into this form."

"But how on earth do we know that? We can hardly start at Aaron A Aaronsen, and go through the phone book?" said Flora.

"I think I know," said George, sadly "Or at least most of it."

Chapter Thirty Seven – What's in a Name?

The fight raged on, Maximus and Earthborn continued to fight, neither seemingly gaining an advantage. Maximus pounded Earthborn's left hand against the wall, until he lost grip of his sword. It fell to the ground, and Maximus kicked it out of the way. It skittered across the floor, and out of the doorway, and clanked as it fell down the spiral stairs.

"How can you possibly know?" asked Flora or George.

"Well, when he spoke to be earlier, there was a reason."

"What?"

"He claims that he knew us before he changed, that when he was killed a few years ago, he was given the choice to come back as he did. And he took it, but only for us."

"Us?" queried Henry.

"Yes, this may be hard to believe, and I am not sure I do yet, but he claims he is, or was, our father."

"What?" cried Henry.

"Never," shouted Flora.

"Really?" said Sir Francis, quietly. "I never saw that coming."

"You don't really believe him do you George?", asked Flora, accusingly "He's a big evil nasty man who has done lots of horrid things."

"But some of it was to protect us. He had to kill Sir Francis, he has been ordered to, and has no choice."

"Who by", demanded Henry.

"That's not important right now. But he tried to save us. Or not kill us at least. We must decide what to do."

"Well", said Sir Francis "the course is clear. We must assume that he is your father, as I assume you know your father's name?"

"I can't remember" said Henry, who was far too young to know him as anything but da-da.

"Yes, well most of it," admitted George.

"His surname was obviously Bannerworth", said Flora.

"And his first name was Dan", continued George.

"So Dan Bannerworth."

"Daniel", corrected Flora "mother always called him Daniel, well when she was annoyed with him."

"So all the time then." Said George, smiling slightly.

"But it must be exact", Sir Francis continued. "Did he have a middle name?"

"I think so, but he never said what it was. I don't think he liked it much."

"Then we are stuck", admitted Varney.

There was another large crash as Earthborn and Maximus continued their struggle.

"Maybe it's an anglegram?" suggested Henry..

"What?"

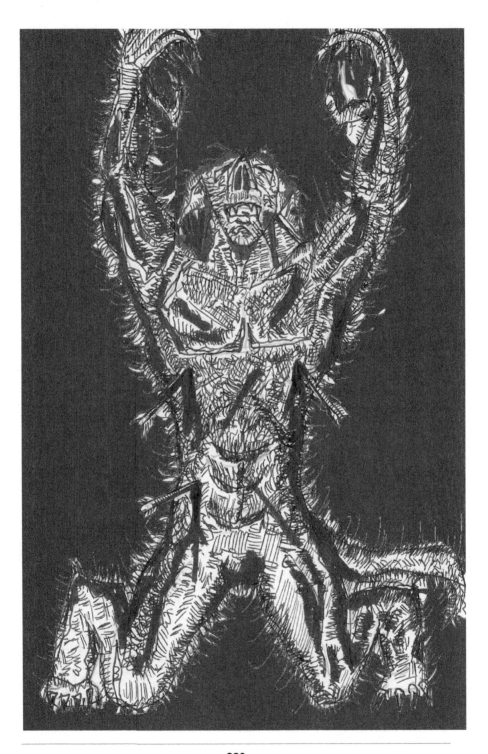

220

"Maybe his name Nathaniel Wayward Earthborn is an anglegram of his real name," Henry continued.

"Ah, an anagram", said Flora.

George thought quickly. "Earthborn, using the letters from that you get BANERORTH. Do you just need another N and a the W and you have Bannerworth. You could be right Henry!"

Henry beamed happily, despite the circumstances.

"Then, you have left ATHANIEL ARDOST", said Flora.

"Take the ANIEL and add the D to it, that's Daniel."

"So what are we left with?"

"ATH AROST"

"Hurry George," said Henry "Maximus is struggling. They all turned and looked. The great rage of Maximus had given him the strength to keep Earthborn at bay, but now he was tiring. Earthborn kicked at him, pushing the wolf back. Then he raised his arm and flexed his wrist, twice. Two ash bolts thudded into the wolf's chest, who howled in pain. Earthborn advanced quickly, sensing the end.

"A Throats, no that's silly. Hattarso. Nope." George closed his eyes and tried to picture the letters in a circle, an old crossword trick. "There's nothing that makes sense."

"It must George, think!"

With that there was a giant yowl, as Maximus was thrown backwards by two more ash bolts. He dropped to the floor, bleeding and breathing shallowly, and then he didn't move.

Earthborn turned and looked at Varney.

"Now for the main event", he said grimly. He reached into his coat pocket, which had been kicked into a corner near him, and drew out a long, pointed stake.

Chapter Thirty Eight – Angels or Daemons

"Well, it has come to this, my friends", smiled Sir Francis at the children. "I fear I can fight him for some time, but I will tire, and he will eventually finish me. But it has been my greatest honour to be called your friend."

With that, he stood up and walked over, placing himself between Earthborn and his own children.

"I believe we have not been officially introduced," said Sir Francis to the tall figure, "I am Sir Francis Percival Varney. And you are?"

"Daniel A. Bannerworth at your service," he said, bowing mockingly.

("A, George, it starts with an A", Flora whispered.

"OK, let me think. That leaves THAROST.")

"Then," continued Sir Francis, "as you are the father of these children, then can I assume that if you destroy me, you will leave them be."

"Of course, vampyr, I never had any wish to hurt them. In fact I have been trying to get back to them for six long years. You have my word."

"The word of?"

"Daniel Bannerworth of course."

"But Daniel A.?"

"Yes Daniel A. I think that is sufficient. Now let us see who will prevail."

With no further words, Bannerworth raised his stake in his good hand, and leveled his crossbow on his burnt hand, and advanced on Varney. Sir Francis floated into the air, and dived down at Bannerworth. They clashed, Varney fighting with fang and claw, Bannerworth with strength and power.

Bannerworth pushed Varney back, and then flexed his right wrist twice. Two bolts thudded into Sir Francis' chest, just missing his heart. Blood started to flow from the wound. Precious blood. Then the fight was once again joined.

Meanwhile George struggled to find a name from the remaining letters.

"ATARTHOS, no. AROTHSTA, doubt it. ASTAROTH?"

"What?" asked Flora

"Astaroth?"

"That sounds familiar," said Flora. "I am sure he was some sort of angel or daemon."

"Well, given we have a man made of clay fighting a vampyr, then our father having a middle name that's either a daemons or angels. That sort of makes sense. So that must be it. What now?"

"We have to write it on a spike, and stick it into his body", said Flora.

"But isn't he our da-da?" asked Henry.

"Maybe. Possibly. Was. I don't know Henry," admitted George.

"OK one thing we do know is Sir Francis is our friend. Even if that is our daddy, then he's no longer human and, let's face it, he's a bit evil", reasoned Flora.

"So we need a spike", said Henry "over there", he pointed. Max was carrying the leather satchel over his shoulder when he changed form, and it had snapped and fallen to the floor. It lay near where Varney and Bannerworth were fighting.

"I'll get it", said Henry.

"But", protested George.

"No, I saw it, and I am the quickest, the smallest", and with that he was gone. He raced across the floor, managing to avoid the struggling pair of Varney and Bannerworth, and scooped up the bag. He scampered back over to George and Flora.

Inside were several spikes. Flora dug one out, and looked in her backpack. She found a silver sharpie, and said "This should do" and started to write on it.

She spelled out "DaNiel AStaroth Bannerworth" on it in silver letters, and blew on it so that it would dry quickly. Then she handed it to George.

"Why me?" asked George.

"Because you will know what to do. You always know what to do," said Flora.

Over the other side of the room, Bannerworth had forced Sir Francis back to the wall, the stake aimed at his heart. Varney looked weak, and had spent all his strength fighting. It was only a matter of moments before Bannerworth would end the fight.

George ran over, the spike in his hand, and stopped just short of Bannerworth. Neither Varney nor his opponent noticed George, who had a clear strike at the broad chest of Bannerworth as he raised his arm to strike at the stricken vampyr.

"What do I do?" he thought to himself "If I do nothing, Sir Francis dies, but my father lives. If I do act, then Sir Francis lives, but I am killing my father."

Chapter Thirty Nine – Such Sweet Sorrow

An arm flew downwards. The sharp point pierced the body, and the creature screamed. It was a sound that no human throat could make. The scream became a thin wail, and then a gurgle. The creature fell backwards, clawing at its body, trying to grab the thing in its chest, the thing that was killing it. It lay on the floor, its arms thrashing, its legs beating the floor. The head whipped from side to side, the jaws opening and closing, with no sound coming from the lips. Then the body started to melt away.

Sir Francis Varney, vampyr of 800 years, looked up at George with sadness in his eyes. After all this time, it had ended like this, in a way he could never have expected. He did not feel regret, just sadness and grief for George, who had made an impossible choice.

Then he slowly stood to his feet, and walked to George's side. The young boy was looking down at his father, who lay on the ground, the seventh spike embedded in the centre of his chest. The silver lettering spelling his name seemed to glow. Tears rolled down George's face, as he suddenly realised the enormity of what he had done. He had killed his father.

Flora and Henry crept over, and cuddled into George to comfort him, but they all found themselves crying.

On the ground, Daniel Astaroth Bannerworth lay there. His flesh started to melt away, like earth in a rainstorm, as his unnatural body started to return to its natural state. That of mud and clay. All three children knelt down by the body, and held hands. George reached out and touched his father's shoulder, but it was now more liquid than solid.

"I am sorry, father, but I did what I thought was best. I followed my heart."

Bannerworth looked back up at him, his eyes starting to float away with the sludge.

"My son" he gurgled, as his human-esque vocal chords started to break down "youu did what wass right. This was noo life foor me. It wass barely exissting. I did what I wanted tooo dooo, all that I was able too doo, and saw yoou all again. Yoou all make me sooo very proooud."

"Is there nothing we can do, Sir Francis?" asked Flora, tears streaming down her face.

Sir Francis shrugged, uncertain.

"Yoou may have destrooyed this boody, buutt theyy still have my soulll. They maaay remakee mee, as theyyy caann while they stillll own my soulll. Stoop them. Dooo not let themm use meee again."

"What, who has your soul?" asked George, urgently. He sensed his father did not have long.

"I cannooot tellll, it is forbiddeeen. But knooow this. I lovvvvvvvvvvvvv-"

And with that, Bannerworth's face fell in, and all life left his body.

The kids cuddled each other, and cried.

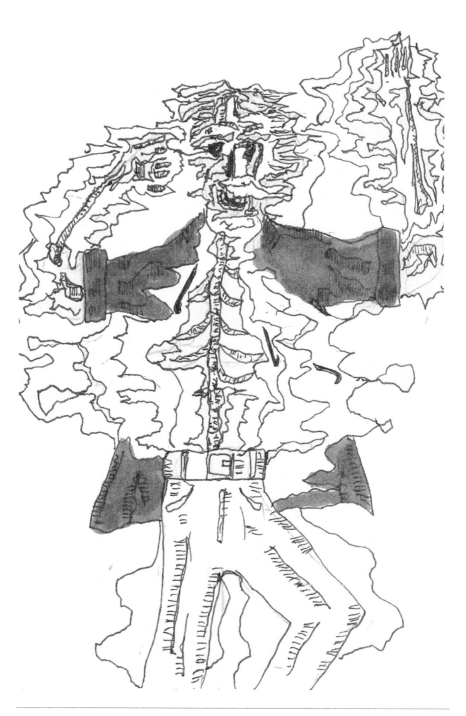

Chapter Forty —After Midnight

Sir Francis left the children to grieve, and walked over to where a huge figure lay still on the ground.

"He looks like a giant rug", thought Varney to himself sadly. Then he knelt down next to his old friend. Maximus was still in wolf form. His body was matted with blood from numerous injuries. Sir Francis reached down, and pulled the wooden crossbow shafts from the huge torso. Blood dripped from the wounds.

He listened closely, and looked with his vampyr eyes, and could see that there was a pulse, albeit weak and erratic. Sir Francis reached over and grabbed Bannerworth's coat.

"It is hardly like he will need it anymore" he thought. He ripped the coat into strips, and started to apply pressure to Maximus' wounds.

"The irony," thought the vampyr "Here I am, mopping up blood with a rag. Barely a year ago I would be lapping it up instead," he reflected. He quickly dressed the worst of Maximus' wounds, and stemmed the most serious bleeding.

"Lycan are tough beasts," he thought to himself. "With rest he will soon be back to his normal, irritating self. Ruining the furniture and turning the grass yellow."

Maximus turned his great head. His amber eyes flickered open and met with Varney's but then closed again. Then he started to breathe deeply. Varney placed the rest of the coat over Maximus to keep him warm.

Happy that he had done what he could, Sir Francis got back to his feet and walked back over to the kids. In front of them was now just a puddle of mud, in a vaguely human form, like in the cartoons when someone runs through a wall. All that was left were the jeans and boots.

George looked up at Sir Francis.

"Thank you, my boy," said the vampyr simply "that cannot have been an easy decision."

"No it wasn't, Sir Francis, but what did father mean?"

"I do not know. I think that is a question for another day. Or night."

"Oh no" cried Flora, "What will mummy think? It's after midnight, and here we are in an old castle."

"Ah, yes," agreed George "we'll think of something," he continued, unsurely.

"How is Maximus?" asked Henry, nervously.

"He is very weak, but he is tough. I think he will be fine, Henry", replied Sir Francis "but we need to get him home. He needs a lot of rest."

"Back to Ratpole?"

"I think not, as it may not yet be safe."

Sir Francis bent and picked up the giant wolf as if he was a baby. It all looked rather absurd. The stick thin vampyr carrying a giant eight foot wolf.

"We can't walk through town like this, Sir Francis. Someone is bound to notice."

"I concur, and this is not as easy as it looks, but we may not have to. It may be that it is quite convenient that we ended up here."

"Why?"

"Well, if I am correct, then we may have an easier way of moving him. I recognised something on the way up here. Follow me."

It was difficult for Varney to carry Maximus down the thin spiral staircase, back into the courtyard, but somehow he managed. When the got there, Sir Francis pointed with his long thin chin. His long thin hands were busy supporting the huge wolf.

"Look at that" he gestured.

"What?" said George.

"On that pillar there. Can you not see, marked into the stone"

In the stone were several marks, intersecting each other in some sort of pattern.

"It's just a bit of graffiti, Sir Francis."

"Ah, is it indeed? Perchance, try pressing the two stones either side."

"What?" said Flora.

"OK", said Henry and he reached up and pushed the stones, which rather unexpectedly slid into the wall. There was a rumbling sound, and a section of the wall slid aside.

"A secret passage", cried Henry, excitedly.

"Another one?" said Flora "how original."

Henry looked inside the dark hole. "There's some stairs downwards."

"Downwards we go, then" said Sir Francis. Again this was a challenge as these stairs were even narrower than the spiral steps. But somehow they arrived at the bottom. In front of them was a tunnel. In the tunnel were two iron rails, and on the rails were a couple of carts.

"An underground railway" said Flora, rather impressed.

"Cool", cried Henry. Yes, Henry also loved trains.

"I recognized the sigil on the wall when I arrived. It is the same one that is over the entrance to the railway under my current abode. I surmise that this track should take us to safety, below the streets"

"What?" asked Henry.

"He saw the sign, and realised there was a rail track under the castle", explained George.

"Ah, why didn't he just say that?"

Varney ignored that, and placed Maximus carefully in the first cart. He pushed at it, and it rolled quite freely. The children jumped into the second cart, and before they knew it, they were travelling below the streets, Varney pushing them as he floated along behind them.

Chapter Forty One – Close Encounters

A couple of days later, most things had calmed down. Mr. March had managed to convince Mrs. Bannerworth that it had been his fault that the kids were out after midnight. George was not convinced that mother was convinced, but she let it go surprisingly easily.

Sir Francis was still holed up in the smugglers den, as Ratpole House still had people camped out looking for UFOs. The crowds had thinned, but Tuesday could be seen at the front, with about twenty other die-hard true believers. The house had done itself proud, and none of the crowd had managed to get inside the old manor.

Late that afternoon, one of the last in the summer holidays, they all sat in the den, trying to work out how to reclaim Ratpole House.

"You cannot stay here indefinitely, Sir Francis. All the stuff to make glood is in the kitchen, and there's no fridge or electricity to keep it cool or warm it up", said George. They had got into the habit of delivering fresh body temperature glood to Sir Francis twice a day – but when school went back on Tuesday, then that would be more difficult.

"I agree, George, my boy. But what can I do?"

"Scare them off, go all super-vampyr on them one night?" suggested Henry.

"No, most assuredly not", cried Sir Francis.

"That's not going to help, Henry. Then there will be just a group of locals with torches and stakes outside," replied Flora.

"Awwww". Henry had enjoyed watching Sir Francis in all his power. It was a bit scary but also kinda cool. Almost as cool as diggers.

They learnt the following day what exactly had happened to Sir Francis at the castle. Mr. March had previously worked as a porter in the local hospital, and had managed to sneak in and borrow (OK, steal) three litres of fresh blood. This had given Varney the power to fight Bannerworth. However, Sir Francis had once again sworn off real blood.

But the problem of Ratpole still remained.

"So what do we do?" asked George.

"Maybe they will just get bored and leave?" suggested Mr. March.

"I doubt it, Maximus. They seem to be a beacon for all things paranormal, and people are arriving daily. Not in great numbers, but if this continues there will be a permanent camp in my front garden."

"It's a shame, that if they want UFOs, that we can't give them UFOs", said Henry quietly.

Mr. March looked around sharply, staring at Henry.

"Henry, that's brilliant. Leave it with me!" he shouted, and ran out of the den.

"Where's he off to?" asked Flora.

"Ah, Maximus does like to surprise people. I am sure we will find out soon enough."

"Sir Francis?" asked George

"Yes, my boy?"

"I was wondering something. Vampyr's cannot go onto hallowed ground without being massively weakened?"

"Yessssss?"

"Then how come in the abbey at the castle, it didn't affect you?"

"Ah, a matter of history, my boy. As long as there have been humans, there has been religion. Whenever there is religion, there are places of worship–"

"Churchs, circles of trees, stone rings?" asked Flora.

"Just so. So if every place that had been used as a place of worship was still harmful to me, then there would be so many places I would not be able to go. But over time, if no one continues to worship at that site, then the effect reduces until it is negligible. That chapel had not been used for worship for hundreds of years – and I could feel that."

"So you could sense it was once a place of worship."

"Yes, I got a sort of itching between my toes, a bit like athlete's foot."

George didn't ask how Sir Francis knew what athlete's foot felt like.

"So, father assumed that any hallowed ground would work?"

"Yessss, indeed. Bit of an amateur error really for a vampyr hunter, but then again he was never–", Varney stopped in mid-sentence when he saw how upset the children were. Sometimes he forgot how important these family relationships were to humans.

"–So the chapel was just a room. The cross was only a carved object."

"Can we do anything about Da-Da?" asked Henry, a lump in his throat.

"We will have to see. Maybe–"

But then Mr. March barged into the room.

"Come, quickly, you are going to love this", he shouted excitedly. "Don't worry, its dusk outside. You should be fine Sir Francis."

They all followed the excited lycan, who loped ahead of them, beckoning them on. They arrived outside Ratpole House a few minutes later. They stood back in the shadows, and watched.

At the front of the house, a small camp had sprung up in the garden. There were tents and a couple of people were lighting fires. There was a smell of BBQ food. Placards were stuck in the ground, or discarded on the grass. Tuesday had somehow managed to get his camper van through the gate, onto the grass, and Sir Francis clenched his fists in annoyance when he saw the mess the tyres had made of his lawn.

"What the? That idiotic human! I have just had that lawn re-laid! I will-"

"Wait, Sir Francis, it's almost time. You are going to like this. Look up."

The late summer sun had just dropped under the horizon, and all was in shadows. Lighting came from street lamps, fires and camera phones. Then there was a humming noise, a deep throbbing sound that seemed to pulse through everyone's bodies. Then all of a sudden, everything went dark.

The street lights winked off, the fires were extinguished, phones all of a sudden had their batteries drained and shut down. The darkness was absolute and not natural, especially as it was still just dusk.

Then there was a thrumming of music in the sky. Four notes played out, reverberating through the sky. Then, directly over Ratpole, a beam of bright light lit up the house. It came down from a dark shape that was hovering in the sky, directly over the old house. It was flat, and disc shaped, and had circular lights around the edge. The outside disc seemed to spin around the inside of the vessel. Or object.

"It's a UFO!" cried Flora, excitedly.

"Well, I suppose to you it is.", smiled Mr. March.

"Of course it is, it's unidentiflied, it's flying, and it's an object!", agreed Henry.

"Just watch", whispered Mr. March.

In the column of light that was shining down from the UFO (or maybe an IFO if you are Mr. March), two figures seemed to descend from the vessel. They were tall and incredibly thin. They had oversized heads, and long fingers. Their eyes were huge and slanted upwards, and oval in shape. They stepped out of the beam. They appeared to be a green-blue colour.

The first creature started talking. Somehow it was amplified in octophonic sound all around so everyone could hear it clearly.

"GREETINGS, EARTHLINGS, WE ARE TRAVELLERS FROM A GALAXY FAR FAR-"

He stopped and listened to his colleague.

"What, don't use that? OK. OK. I suppose it is a bit obvious. Very well.."

"WE COME FROM A GALAXY A LONG LONG WAY AWAY. A REALLY LONG LONG LONG WAY AWAY. WE HAVE TRAVELLED HERE FROM OMERCRON PER-."

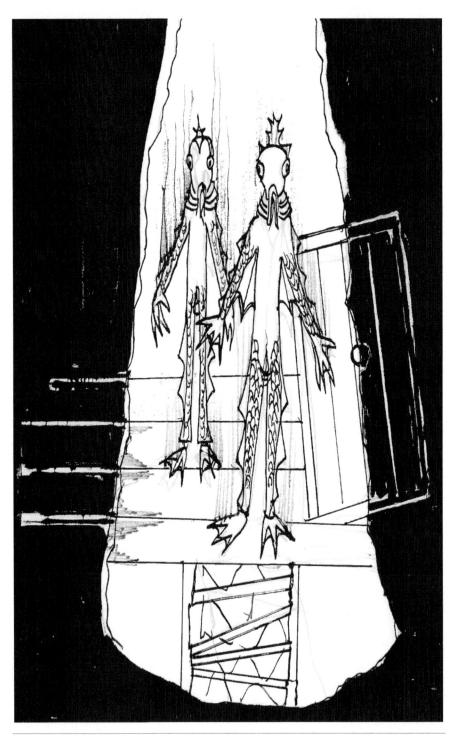

His colleague tugged at his (or her) elbow and leaned in to whisper to him.

"What, you think they will know that as well? Oh blast.

"HUMANITY, WE HAVE TRAVELLED FROM THE PLANET-"

She (or he) stopped again and whispered "can I used Skaro? Gallifrey? Vulcan? No. Hmmm. I'll have to improvise."

"WE HAVE TRAVELLED FROM A PLANET THAT CANNOT BE PRONOUNCED IN YOUR SIMPLISTIC LANGUAGE AND WE HAVE COME TO RECLAIM OUR KIN, WHO HAS BEEN TRAPPED HERE FOR MANY OF YOUR HUMAN YEARS. THE VISITOR WHO LIVES HERE WILL TRAVEL BACK HOME WITH US AND WE WILL BOTHER YOU NO FURTHER. BUT BE WARNED, LEAVE THIS PLACE AND DO NOT RETURN, OR WE WILL DESTROY IT AND YOU!"

They turned and walked back into the beam.

"BYE BYE", said one of the alien visitors, waving happily as he/she/it walked back into the beam.

The figures disappeared back up the beam of light which then shut off. The lights around all came back on, and with a HMMMMMMM noise, the disc like ship flew away.

"OH, SORRY" came the amplified voice again "WE FORGOT SOMETHING."

Once more the lights went out, and the large ship returned into view. It hovered over the centre of the camp.

"AS YOU EARTHLINGS SEEK TO LEARN MORE ABOUT OUR KIND, WE WILL TAKE ONE OF YOU WITH US. WE HAVE CHOSEN!"

Once more the beam lit up, but this time it focused down on Tuesday. He looked up, his hair blown off his head, and stood arms out. His face was half terrified, half excited. Then, the light picked him up and transported him up to the ship. The light blinked out again.

"BYE BYE. WE WONT BE BACK AGAIN."

"Play the music again. Yes that one", said the voice again.

The four notes once more reverberated through the sky. And then the ship was gone. Once more, all the lights came back on.

On the ground it was chaos. Everyone grabbed their bags, trampling over tents and placards, and terrified they ran out of the gate. A few minutes later, all that was left of the camp was a few flattened tents, and Tuesday's camper van.

"What, you got a UFO to abduct him?" marveled George to Mr. March.

"Of course not. That was just some of Kazim's friends from Archive Eight. They were also visiting Mr. H. That ship they use to travel underwater, but they can also fly, as you have seen."

"And the aliens were normal people in costumes?"

"No, Archive Eight is underwater, and some of the people who live there are amphibian. They volunteered to do this. They thought it would be a bit of a laugh. Of all the Archives, those at Eight are by far the most fun."

"So what are they going to do with Tuesday?" asked Flora, "Take him back to their Archive?"

"No no. they are just going to fly around really really fast until he gets dizzy. Then they will pretend to do some operations on him. Don't worry, they won't hurt him, but they will pretend to embed something in his teeth. In reality they will give him a good clean, scale and polish. They have excellent dental care. Tuesday will never need another filling again."

"But then what?"

"After a while, they will drop him off in a field in the middle of nowhere, but close enough so he can easily walk to safety. They'll probably change his watch so it says a different date and time, maybe dye his hair white so it looks like he has aged 10 years overnight. Stuff like that. When he tries to tell anyone, no one will believe him."

"But what about what just happened. There will be photos, videos-"

"No, of course there won't! That beam of light rendered all cameras and recording devices inoperative. No one will have a thing." Mr. March sounded rather pleased with himself.

They looked down at the now empty grounds of Ratpole House.

"It appears you can go home again, Sir Francis." said George happily.

"Indeed, I have missed the old house." smiled Sir Francis, grotesquely.

Epilogue – Dead Men Walking

In a nearby grey city, under a grey sky, is a grey building. It seems both tall and squat, and wide and tall, and looms ominously on the skyline.

The building is all concrete with small glass windows. There are no signs outside the building, and just one set of double-doors in. Workers trudge in, grey men and women, wearing grey suits and carrying grey briefcases. The workforce arrives at 7am, and leave at 11pm, every day, weekends included.

Through the double-doors there is no reception, as no one ever visits the building who doesn't work there. No one would want to. On the wall, there is a simple sign on grey stone, reading,

"ROMERO, JACKSON AND SAVINI"

There are no elevators, just concrete stairs that go up and up seemingly forever. The grey men and women troop up the concrete stairs and file off into their offices. Each of the first 13 floors is one giant office, with rows and rows of desks. Small, thin desks, arranged in neat rows and isles. Trolleys are pushed up and down these rows and isles, and workers place thick card files on desks as they go, whilst others collect completed files.

The workers are at their desks at 7am exactly. The workers take a file, from the in tray, open it, and then work through it. They enter numbers into old calculators, the type that have a paper roll coming out of them. The whole room is filled with the clack-clack-clack of calculator keys, and the burrr-burrr-burrr of the printers.

There are no computers in the office. No music, no water fountains, no toilets, no coffee cups on desks. There is no chatter, no one talks, they just work. Soon, the floor is full of curls of paper from the calculators.

At 12 noon, a siren rings, and on each floor, a row at a time, the workers trudge out of a door into the canteen area. They eat from a limited and rather unique menu in the grey canteens. They moan in anticipation as they queue up for their meals, and then eat quickly. Each are back at their desks within 15 minutes.

Up on the 14th floor, there are separate offices. The 14th office is a large office. It's a drab office, with lead coloured walls and ashen carpet.

Dominating the room is a large grey desk, its has files of paper files stacked on it, covering most of the top. Behind the desk sits a woman.

She has grey hair, cut in a rather severe grey bob that only reaches halfway down her face. She's studiously reading a file, when there is a knock on the door.

"Enter", she says in a low monotonous tone.

The door opens and a grey man shuffles in.

"Yes, Arthur?", asks the woman.

"There is a case here, I think you should look at". There is no small talk.

He hands a thick file over the desk. The grey lady opens it and reads through it, examining the ticker-tape like rolls of paper.

"This being, he has never paid tax?"

"No."

"Nothing under the Act of Making Good the Deficiency of Clipped Money Act of 1696?"

"The window tax? No."

"How many windows?"

"Over 20."

"So 10 shillings per week is owed until 1850?"

"Yes. A total of £26.207.40 is owed."

"Plus compound interest?"

"Of course. So that makes it £34,002,130.03. Approximately."

"Is that all?" the grey lady asked

"No. That's just the start"

"Income tax since 1798?"

"Nothing."

"Purchase tax? Poll tax? Council Tax?"

"No. No. No."

The grey lady almost smiles.

"Interesting. Have to a final number?"

The man hands over a single page of typed paper.

"Hmmm. So he owes the State £456,674,307."

"And?"

"56p. My apologies, ma'am."

"We must be precise in these matters, Arthur."

"Yes."

"Excellent. Then start proceedings. Assign a retrieval team."

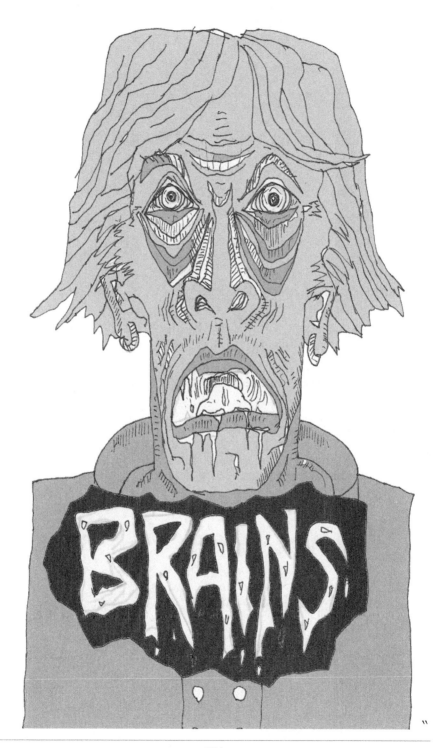

Very good."

"What's the name of the "client"?"

"Varney. Sir Francis Varney."

She looks at her watch. It's made of battleship grey stainless steel.

"Hmmm, 12 noon. Lunch time. Do you know what's on today's specials at the canteen?"

"Yes, brains on toast"

The grey lady's grey eyes light up, turning red in anticipation.

"OOOHHHH, BRAAAAINNNSSSSS"

She stands up, and they both leave the office, moaning to themselves, and walking stiffly towards the canteen.

"BRAAINNNS, BRAIINNNS, BRAIINNNNS", they both moan as they walk.

To find out what happens next, look out for:

Varney the Vampyr
Book 3: Zombie Debt Eaters

Race Around Ratpole

A Bonus Adventure starring (former) Professor Chillingworth

WARNING: Contains spoilers about Varney the Vampyr Book Two!

The villainous Earthborn (aka Vampyr Hunter B) stole a lot of small items from the Bannerworth's house and tried to frame Professor Chillingworth (aka Chili) with the thefts. However three items were not recovered from 99 Shackledown Road. They all belonged to Flora, who is very upset. Can you help Chili to try to find them to cheer Flora up?

You choose which route Chili takes – but beware! There may be anything (or anyone!) around any corner. The old house has a surprising amount of residents. Some may help you, some may hinder you.

A piece of paper, a pencil and an eraser may be useful as Ratpole House is easy to get lost in! There is also an **ADVENTURE SHEET** that you can use to keep track of things.

For this adventure, you will also need 2 six sided dice. One six sided dice will be called 1d6; two will be called 2d6.

Each section you read, you will be given a choice. For example, if you want to turn left, go to Section 15. If you want to turn right, go to Section 31. So if you choose to turn right, then you turn to the paragraph that starts with the number 31.

The only thing you need to work out now is Chili's **STAMINA**. If this gets to 0, then you must turn straight to section **111**. To work out his **STAMINA** roll 1 dice, and add 6 to the score. You should have a **STAMINA** of between 7 and 12.

When you are asked to check and ability such as **AGILITY** or **OBSERVANCE**, there is a **DIFFICULTY** level. The higher the **DIFFICULTY**, the harder the task! All you do is roll 2d6. If you roll the more than the **DIFFICULTY** level, then you have been successful. If you roll less or equal to the **DIFFICULTY** then you have failed that task.

You may also be given some Codewords – record those on your **ADVENTURE SHEET**.

Oh and by the way, some of the things you may learn may be true, mostly true, partly true (but mostly false) or downright balderdash!
Good luck – you may need it!

Adventure Sheet

Use a pencil or photocopy this sheet

Stamina	1d6+6
Current Stamina	

If Stamina gets to 0,
TURN
TO 111 !

Time	12
Current Time	

If Time gets to 0,
TURN
TO 33 !

Flora's Items
(Tick box if found)

Gold Ring	
Silver Necklace	
Copper Bracelet	

If you have all 3 items ticked,
TURN TO 100 !

Items in Bag
(Maximum of 5 items)

Codewords
Record any Codewords you are given here!

Star Locations

1

Flora sat on her bed in her room, a frown creasing her face. Chili, her small green possibly immortal flying squirrel, sat perched on the headboard. He stared with liquid black eyes at Flora, feeling Flora's pain. Chili was devoted to Flora, and anything that upset her, upset him. This was some change from the evil Professor that tried to achieve life eternal a few short months ago.

Chili remembered all of this, and all of his past life as the erstwhile Professor. When he thought back on his pre-Sciuridaen life, it was almost like he was looking at his past life through someone else's eyes. He knew that the tall, thin man with the crazy hair was him, but he realised one thing. He didn't like The Professor – as he tended to call himself from his human days.

He felt no urge to turn back to human – or vampyr now – and he hadn't even tried. He may have been able to, as no-one really knew the long term effects of being caged in silver. But even if he could turn back, he realised he really didn't want to.

As The Professor, he had been arrogant, aloof and a complete ass. He had no family, no friends, only henchmen/women/creatures. He had become so obsessed in trying to life forever that he had completely forgotten what it was like to live at all.

Now Chili had a family, albeit a strange family. His previous foe, Sir Francis Varney, was now a friend, as was the wolf-man Maximus March. Chili split his time between the rambling Ratpole House, and the more modern 99 Shackledown Road. He liked spending time at Ratpole, but he loved it at 99. The main reason was the kids, George, Henry, and especially Flora.

He had a mildly antagonistic relationship with Mrs. Bannerworth, who mostly tolerated Chili. The main issue was that Chili could be a bit of a sneak, and tended to think with his stomach, and so he liked to raid the pantry and the fridge after midnight. No child locks on the fridge could stop him, as despite his diminutive size and lack of opposable thumbs, Chili had lost none of his human intelligence. After all he was a scientific genius who had managed to isolate the vampyric secret to immortality. Nothing Mrs. Bannerworth could do would stop him from mounting his midnight raiding parties on the kitchen.
Flora sighed and spoke, for the first time in a while,

"It's not fair Chili, I know you didn't steal all the stuff that we found in your cage, and it was that horrid Earthborn-"

(Flora was still not convinced that Earthborn had been / still is (Delete as applicable) Daniel Bannerworth, her father – long-time assumed to be dead)

"-But I am still missing a few things. My gold ring, that mummy got me for Christmas; my favourite silver necklace that Grandy gave me; and a copper bracelet that Nanny bought me. I am sad that I can't find them, and I have looked everywhere in the house."

Chili realised that people often misjudged Flora, as she liked sparkly objects and shiny trinkets. She did, but she also liked where she got them from as it reminded her of the people she loved. Chili's little heart went out to Flora, and he resolved to find these three objects.

"It's so sad as I have a party straight after school, and I was hoping to wear my bestest things. But I can't find the ring, the necklace and the bracelet anywhere". Flora looked very sad.

They clearly were not at No 99. And so Chili thought "Maybe Earthborn hid some objects in Ratpole House to incriminate me"

So he resolved to spend the night at Ratpole, and search for these items. Hopefully, by the time Flora woke in the morning, he could present them to her and cheer her up. But it would have to be before she left for school as she was taking her party clothes with her.

He spent the next couple of hours with Flora until it was bed time, and then he chirped at her, gave her a cuddle, and climbed up and out of the open window, and headed to Ratpole House.

Turn to **3**

2

"Hmm, let me think. Ah, my memory never fails me. I have seen a silver necklace around the neck of a recent resident in the house. They live in hidden in the dark. But beware, it can be a bit sticky getting to see them.

But I do remember them saying that they were very fond of it, but what they really wanted was a hairbrush. I think I will go back to my portrait now to read for a while and recharge my ectoplasm"

How a ghost can read a book is beyond Chili (and you) but Steeple turns around the flies back into the portrait.

Turn to **57** and choose something else to do in this room

3

Chili scampered across and down the road towards Ratpole House. The sun was just about to pass under the horizon, and darkness was falling quickly. The house, raised up on a hill at the end of the road, loomed over the end of the road, veiled in shadow. Chili quickly ran up the side of the outer wall and jumped to the nearest tree trunk. He climbed up quickly and ran from tree to tree, branch to branch, until he arrived at the front of Ratpole House

It is now not long before the sun will rise, and Flora will be awake and leaving for school. Your **TIME** is recorded on your **ADVENTURE SHEET**, as starting at 12. This is how many **TIME** points you have. If you get to 0 before finding all three items and getting them back to Flora, then you will have failed in your mission.

Note down the number **33**. If you're **TIME** score gets to 0, then you must turn to section **33** straight away.
You will need to find these items
Gold Ring
Silver Necklace
Copper Bracelet
As you find these items, put a tick next to it on your **ADVENTURE SHEET**. You may want to draw a map of your progress as you go – as Ratpole House can be tricksy!
You also have a little bag that Chili has over his shoulder in case he finds Flora's precious items (or anything else). The bag can hold up to 5 items.

Turn to **43**

4

Chili is a bit nervous and looking forward into the dark, and he doesn't really pay attention to the ceiling above him. As he walks into the tunnel, the threads hanging from the roof start to snag in his fur. They are sticky, and Chili tries to brush them off, but every time he does, he gets more tangled. Soon he is close to panicking and he thrashes around with his sharp claws, trying to cut his way through. But the threads seem to constrict, and pull him off the ground until he is dangling a couple of feet off the floor.

Then Chili hears a click-click-click-click-click sound. It sounds like many small feet are closing in on him. Turn to **20**

5

Chili scampers over to the wall, and looks up and sees that above him, there's a lamp in a wall sconce. Chili can see that there are some scuff marks on the wall, which makes it look like the lamp has moved. He jumps up, and hangs from the lamp. His weight on the fixture means that it starts to turn around, clockwise. It moves initially very slowly, but then speeds up and is spins around at 180 degrees.

At the same time there is a click underneath Chili, and two of the floorboards drop open on hinges, creating a one metre square hole in the floor. The speed of the rotation of the lamp throws Chili off the fitment, and he drops down towards the dark hole that's now underneath him. Chili cries out, a shrill little cry as he falls flailing. He tries to stretch out his arms so that he can glide down the hole, but he hits the wall of the hole and then bounces form side to side down a dark brick chute. Eventually a flap opens below Chili, and he flies out of the house, landing firmly on the ground by the front door.

Lose 2 **STAMINA** points and 1 **TIME**

Turn back to **43** and choose another way to get into the house.

6

"Ah, that is most disappointing. You cannot have been paying attention during the adventures earlier on – as the children most definitely know my name. However if you do happen to remember it, maybe if you come back I will help you. Little happens in this house that I am not aware of"

Then the sprightly spirit turns and flies back into the portrait, and Chili is left in the room alone.

Lose 1 **TIME** point
Turn to **57** and choose a different option. You cannot look at the portrait
again this time in the room.

7

Chili sits on the floor, rubbing his backside. The creature cut the threads
above that were suspending Chili in the air. Lose 2 **STAMINA** points.
Chili frees himself of the remainder of the threads, which seem to have lose
their stickiness now they have been snipped. He stands up and stares at
the creature.

"Oh, we is most sorry" says the creature, *"We did not mean to hurt you.
But we must reset our traps if we want to eat."*

It looks closer at Chili, its multifaceted eyes gleaming.
*"Ah, now we recognise you. You are the curious creature we have seen
recently. You passed through here with some of the humanes, is that not
what they are called. We have recently just moved into this lovely dank
tunnel. Did Sir Francis not say? But we mean you no harm. We are named
Wormald, and we are an Aranesape. We thought you were a ratty at first,
a ratty with a silly tail, when we saw you, and we likes to eat rattys, but
it seems not"*

Chili shakes his head enthusiastically before Wormald could ever think he
was a rat. **TEST CHILI'S OBSERVANCE** with a **DIFFICULTY** of 8.
If you roll 9 or more, turn to **27**
If you roll 8 or less, turn to **90**

8

Chili walks over to the chair. It looks so comfy and Chili is quite tired. He
jumps up on it and curls up. It's even more comfortable that it looked and
soon Chili is gently snoring.

Lose 3 **TIME** points.
Now turn to **25** and choose again.

9

*"Ah yes! I have seen a golden ring, one that I knew did not belong here. Last I saw
it, it was in the possession of Morris. You can find the entrance to his "rooms" in
the entrance hall, if you look closely. But beware, Morris can be a bit bullish. But
that is all I have to tell. I think I will go back to my portrait now for a rest. The
warm fire makes me sleepy"*

How a ghost can be sleepy is beyond Chili (and you) but Steeple turns around the flies back into the portrait.

Turn to **57** and choose something else to do in this room

10

The star Chili stepped on is a transport spell, which moves Chili to another area of Ratpole House, if you know the section for that area.

Write down **SECOND FLOOR BEDROOM = 85** as you may need it later.

This time, Chili find himself in the second floor bedroom.
If you haven't been to this room before, read the text first. If you have been there, then look at the picture opposite **57**, and choose what you want Chili to do next.

Turn to **57**

11

Chili pulls the plug from green bottle with his claw and it hisses slightly.
He lifts the bottle to his nose and smells. It smells of green grass, herbs and spices and the mere smell is invigorating. Chili lifts it to his lips and drinks it down in one. It is delicious. It a potion of **STAMINA**.

If Chili has lost any **STAMINA**, then you can increase his **STAMINA** back up by 1d6 points – but not past his original score.

If Chili has yet to lose any **STAMINA**, then firstly well done! But secondly, the next time you are told Chili has lost **STAMINA** you can ignore it – as the potion is still working. But only one time!

Feeling much refreshed, turn to **25** and make another choice.

12

Nervously, Chili creeps into the hole. **TEST CHILI'S OBSERVANCE** with a **DIFFICULTY** of 9

If you roll 10 or more, turn to **23**
If you roll 9 or less, turn to **4**

13

In his haste to turn and run, Chili runs straight into several of the threads that hang from the ceiling. They snag him and stick to his fur. He tries to fight, but the fight turns into panic as the threads seem to tighten around him. Soon he can hardly move, and the threads contract and pull him off the floor. He hangs there helplessly

Turn to **87**

14

The green door is closed, and the handle is in the centre of the wide door, about three feet up. Chili stands on his hind legs and is able to reach the door knob with his small hands. He grabs it and hangs there, swinging. The door knob is still and hard to turn, especially when Chili is hanging from it. You will have to **TEST CHILI'S STRENGTH**.

The door has a **STRENGTH** of 5
Roll 2 six sided dice (which will now be called 2d6) and add up the numbers. If you rolled 6 or more, you are strong enough and the door swings open and inwards. Then turn to **28**
If you rolled 5 or less, then Chili fails to open the door.

You will have to find another way in. lose 1 **TIME** point. You can either get Chili to:
Via the cellar door, turn to **19**
Via the broken window, turn to **21**
If you have tried all 3 ways to get in and failed at each, turn to **73**

15

"Ah, very good, very good. The simple thing I want to know is "What is my name?""
If you can remember the name of this pesky phantom (and you should know it!), then take the first two letters of his name and convert them to numbers (A=1, B=2, ..., Y=25, Z=26). Add these two numbers together and turn to the number you get.
If you cannot, or do not, know the annoying apparitions name, then turn to **6**

Chili walks along another dark corridor, and there's nothing remarkable about it at all. He considers turning around, and then he notices something round next to one of the columns. He looks and sees it's an inflated beach ball. What a curious thing to find in such a place.

Carefully, Chili picks it up, trying not to puncture the ball with his sharp claws. He manages to pull out the stopper, and squeezes it to deflate it which it does with a "PPPPAAAARRRRPPPP" noise. Once it's empty of air. Chili folds it and places it in his bag.

Write down **BEACH BALL** and the Codeword "**BOUNCY**" on your **ADVENTURE SHEET**.

Turn to **69** and choose again.

17

Slowly, and rather uncomfortably, as Sir Francis is still sat in the bath naked, Chili gets his points across.

"Ah, my dear Professor, I fear I do not have Maximus' or Floras' gift for understanding you. I am afraid that I cannot help you, and I am busy. After my bath I have to do my mindfulness exercises and my stretching."

As well as baths, Sir Francis had recently discovered that meditation and stretching relaxed him, especially before bed. And especially after the recent unfortunate incident. He had even tried tantric breathing, but he found that pretty impossible as he doesn't breathe.

Now that is all I know, and so could you please leave me to my ablutions. And please do not tell the others."

Chili puts his thumb up to say he won't, or tries to. Then he realises he doesn't have an opposable thumb and just nods his head. He turns and leaves the room.

As he does he noticed a wooden hairbrush on a dresser. Obviously Sir Francis has no use for it, and so Chili picks it up and puts it in his bag. Note down that you have a **WOODEN HAIRBRUSH**. Write down the Codeword **TANGLED**

Behind him, the song starts again.

He never ever eats,

So he's as thin as a rake,

And what does he drink?

Well, for Pete's sake

Don't you know by now?
Not water from a spring
Nor milk from a cow
No....Blood is his thing
He'll drink blood from a bat or a rat,
A dog or a horse
A cow or a cat,
Blood from any source
He may even drink
Blood from you
Let's hope
That he never will do
And so if you don't know by now
Let's make it abundantly clear
He is a vampyr
And he has been for many a year
But he was all alone
And really lonely and sad
All the people he's drunk
Are making him feel bad
So he sits all alone
Every evening in his house
All by himself
Well, except the occasional mouse"

To be honest, the lyrics of the song are not much better than the voice
singing it. Chili is relieved as he walks away. However you have wasted
some time, and so lose 1 **TIME** point.
You can now ask Chili to either
Go straight across the landing to the other door, turn to **63**
Or you can turn to **28** and choose again

18

Chili shrugs to himself and starts head down the wall, his sharp claws
struggle to gain and purchase on the old stones, and they are so tight
fitting there is no mortar between them that he can use to hold onto. Chili
inches down, centimetre by centimetre, but after a couple of near slips, he
finally reaches the hard stone floor.

Turn to **24**

19

Chili heads around to the right of the house and finds the double bulkhead doors into the cellar. These are wooden double doors that are at an angle slanting up from the ground. Chili tests the doors and rattles them, but there is a stout padlock locking the two doors together. Chili will have to try to pick the padlock with his claw. To do this you will have to **TEST CHILI'S DEXTERITY**.

The lock has a **COMPLEXITY** of 6

Roll 2 six sided dice (which will now be called 2d6) and add up the numbers. If you rolled 7 or more, then the lock clicks open. Chili pulls it off the hasp and heaves one of the heavy doors open. Then turn to **62**

If you rolled 6 or less, then Chili fails to open the door. Lose 1 **TIME**. You will have to find another way in. You can either get Chili to:

Through the green door, turn to **14**

Via the broken window, turn to **21**

If you have tried all 3 ways to get in and failed at each, turn to **73**

20

A shadow appears in the tunnel under Ratpole. It's indistinct as first, as it is small and far away, but soon grows in size. The click-click-click-click gets louder as the figure gets closer, and soon echoes around the chamber. **CLICK-CLICK-CLICK-CLICK-CLICK**.

Chili can start to see a shape appearing in the shadow. First he sees two pairs of multi-faceted eyes gleaming in the shadows. Then the figure is clearer. It almost fills the tunnel, which is about 5 foot tall, and seems to brush past the hanging threads unencumbered. It has a human like torso but instead of hands it seems to have pincers.

The noise is made by its several sets of legs, each of which that ends with a spiked claw.

The face is still mainly in shadow. Apart from the eyes, that shine brightly and with a dreadful desire.

Turn to **87**

21

Chili heads around to the left of the house and looks up. A couple of floors up, he can see the broken window. One of the window panes was smashed, and that would be more than enough space for Chili to slip through. However the house has been freshly painted and it will be difficult for even Chili to get a grip to climb up, but he will have to do this. It will be a tricky climb. To do this you will have to **TEST CHILI'S AGILITY**.

The climb requires an **AGILITY** of more than 8.
Roll 2 six sided dice (which will now be called 2d6) and add up the numbers. If you rolled 9 or more, then Chili manages to climb the wall and slip in through the window. Then turn to **57**
If you rolled 8 or less, then Chili fails to climb up the tower and in fact slips and falls the last 10 feet. Lose 2 **STAMINA** and 1 **TIME** point:
Through the green door, turn to **14**
Via the cellar door, turn to **19**
If you have tried all 3 ways to get in and failed at each, turn to **73**

22

To the left of the cellar is what appears to be a large tea box, and an old kid's bike.

The tea box is about a metre square, and was used to carry loose tea leaves in bulk by sea across from Sri Lanka. The box is made of cheap wood, and bound in aluminium at the corners and edges. The metal has become splintered in places, as has the wood, and there are many places to catch an arm or leg on. The top of the chest has been broken in, like when a barrel is hit with a large hammer. Chili cannot see inside as all looks dark. The bike leaning against the tea box has high handlebars that curve back on themselves. It has a small front wheel and a larger rear one. On top of the rear wheel is a long seat with a back made of black plastic. In the centre of the bike is the gear stick, which you have to reach down to change the gear. It's called a Chopper and was very popular with kids in the 1970's.

Do you want Chili to?
Search inside the tea box? Turn to **36**
Try to ride the bike? Turn to **49**

23

Chili walks through the hole into darkness. He's only gone a short way when he notices something worrying. As he looks around with his keen eyes, he notices that the network of fine threads hanging from the ceiling. Chili reaches out a paw and touches one of the strands. It is incredibly sticky and Chili has trouble shaking it from his fur.

He thinks about going back and looks around and sees that he is a few feet into a tunnel. He can see a vague light a couple of metres back.

He checks the other way and sees that the tunnel is dark, but what he can see indicates that it is round, but twists, and made of stone that has been polished smooth. More silken threads hang from the roof of the tunnel as it winds its way under Ratpole House.

Then Chili hears a click-click-click-click-click sound. It sounds like many small feet are closing in on him. Turn to **89**

24

Chili finds himself in the cellar at Ratpole House. He knows this place quite well, although recently there have been strange noises emanating from the cellar – and Sir Francis believes there maybe something nasty in the cellar – so he needs to be careful!

Look at the picture opposite and see what you would like Chili to examine now he is in the cellar, and turn to that number.

25

Chili walks past the old piano on the right hand wall, behind the door, and turns right. He knows this way well, as it's to the kitchen. He scurries along and into the kitchen, but sees nothing of interest. Then he sees some light ahead, through another door off the kitchen and into the parlour. He scampers towards it and enters the room.

It's a cosy comfortable room. As with many in Ratpole house, on the rear wall are some bookcases, and a short cabinet. There is a table, a nice comfy chair, and a high back settee. Look at the picture opposite and see where you want Chili to investigate first.

If you want Chili to leave the room, then turn to **28** and go back to the entrance hall.

26

Chili leaps off the doorstep just as the large door gets too heavy for him –
but he is a bit slow! It slams down and catches his rear end as he starts to
glide down. The impact causes him to tumble end of end in the air, and he
doesn't glide to the ground, he more plummets towards it.

He lands with a thud, and lies there stunned for a while. Reduce Chili's
STAMINA by 4. If his **STAMINA** is now 0 or less, turn to **111**

Otherwise, turn to **24**

27

As Wormald is talking, Chili sees in its matted chest hair there is a glitter
of silver. Its Floras **SILVER NECKLACE.** Chili's heart skips a beat when
he sees it – as it has a distinctive star hanging from it.

He point at it and gesture excitedly, trying not to chirp or "squeak" so he
don't upset Wormald.

*"Oh this trinket, yes we found it when we were tunneling. It seems to have
fallen from the main house, through a gap in the wooden things above, but
it is pretty to our eyes – do you not think so?"*

It takes Chili a while but by a mixture of hand gestures, drawing in the
earth and acting, Chili gets across to Wormald that this valuable to Chili.

*"So it's your friends, and you are trying to get it back for her. That is so
commendable. It is now obvious you are not a ratty with a silly tail. No
ratty would act so honourably. So we definitely will not eat you. But we
regret, we cannot give it to you. In our culture, we must trade gifts. If you
could find something that we would like, then please come back again,
and we can talk. Something to help us look after our hair, maybe. It gets
terribly matted. Otherwise, we have traps to set for rattys if we want to
eat tonight."*

And with that, Wormald turns around and its mandibles start to chatter
together. From the mouth comes long silken threads, which Wormald
expertly gathers and sticks to the ceiling, like a spider would create its
web. It uses the serrated edges on its claws to snip the threads, as it lays its
traps.

It is just as well Chili did not get tangled in the threads or Chili may have
been dinner.

Chili turns and leaves the tunnel. Turn back to **24** and choose again

28

Ahead of Chili was a large open hallway. Two large staircases rose from the left wall and the right wall, up to the first floor, and curved around to meet each other in the centre. A large landing, with high balustrades, looked down over the hall.

Turn to the next page and choose where you want to go in the picture.

29

If you have the Codeword **TANGLED**, maybe you should go another way. Try the tunnel at the left hand side of the cellar.

Otherwise, you decide that Chili should try the stairs up out of the cellar, to explore the rest of the house.

Chili scurries over to the stairs and leaps up them two at a time, his tail swishing. There are 15 steps up. Chili hops up two then two more, then two more, but then his back foot lands on a loose stair board. The board slips backwards, swinging around at its only held by one nail, and Chili staggers.

Then his other back foot comes down where the board used to be and he starts to fall.

TEST CHILI'S AGILITY with a **DIFFICULTY** of 8.
If you roll 9 or more, turn to **53**
If you roll 8 or less, turn to **37**

30

Chili shrugs to himself and starts head down the wall, his sharp claws struggle to gain and purchase on the old stones, and they are so tight fitting there is no mortar between them that he can use to hold onto. Chili inches down, centimetre by centimetre. Then his left front leg slips, when he is about a third of the way down. He is unable to recover his grip, and tumbles towards the hard stone floor.

He lands with a thud and an audible groan. Chili lies there, stunned, for a few moments. Then he sits up, shakes his head to try to stop the stars spinning around it, and dusts himself off. Nothing seems broke, he just feels a bit battered and bruised.

Lose 2 **STAMINA** points. If your **STAMINA** is now 0 or less, turn to **111**
Otherwise, turn to **24**

31

Leaning against the right hand cellar wall is an old battered mattress. Its
yellow with age, and some of its springs have burst through the thinning
material. Its smells musty and a bit of rats wee. Chili can see that there are
some small footprints in the dirt of the cellar floor. They lead towards a
small hole that has been dug into the mattress at its base. It looks like
something may have made a passageway through the mattress. But to
where?
It looks like it is just about big enough for Chili to fit through, as long as he
crawls on his tummy.
If you want Chili to investigate this tunnel, turn to **84**
If not, lose 1 **TIME** and turn to **24** and investigate another area.

32

At the end of the hallway is a cabinet, and one it several candles are
burning.

TEST CHILI'S OBSERVANCE with a **DIFFICULTY** of 7.
If you roll 8 or more, turn to **35**
If you roll 7 or less, turn to **104**

33

Oh no! it's already morning and Flora has left for school. Chili has wasted the evening trying to find all three items, and Flora won't be able to wear them at the party.

Maybe you can try again to see if you can find them in time!

34

Chili pulls the door open and sees the strangest sight. The room is mainly in darkness, but the floor is alive with small creatures. They are each only about 6 inches tall, and seem to have no arms, and short stumpy legs. On top of the legs are rectangular bodies with no visible arms that end with a curved dome of a head. Each has two eyes, a slit for a nose, and small lipless mouths, that are filled with small pointed teeth. They are all different colours, red, blue, green and even yellow. They are Bunions, a strange type of creature that sometimes appear for a few days and then leave without a trace.

They are all jumping up and down on the floor excitedly, and chirping away to themselves and each other in delight. It looks like a floor full of animated Smarties as they fling themselves around. They all seem to be looking upwards and so Chili follows their line of sight.
In the air is a glimmering circlet of metal, spinning through the air. It gleams with a warm reddish colour in the dim light. As the ring flies through the air a Bunion leaps up and catches it in their mouth, lands and them jumps back up, somehow spinning their body. The ring flies across the room and another Bunion leaps and catches it.
Chili recognises the circlet. Its Flora's copper bracelet!
If you want Chili to try to catch the bracelet, turn to **82**
If you have anything that would get the Bunions attention, turn to **95**

35

As Chili examines the candles flickering, his eyes are drawn towards the wall to the left of the flames. In between two wooden beams there seems to be an outline of something oblong and about 6 feet tall. Above this are what appears to be a pair of horns attached to the wall.

Chili scampers up the left wooden beam, and jumps over onto the horns. He grabs them with his front paws and hands there. As he does, they start to move forward as if on a hinge, so that the top of the horns start to lean out from the wall. There is an audible "click" and a creaking below Chili. Then he feels a breeze ruffling his fur. He looks down and sees a door has swung open beneath the horns – that was the oblong shape in the wall – a hidden door!

Chili drops lightly to the floor and heads into the darkness behind the door.

There's a corridor that leads downwards for about a few dozen feet, and then it opens up into a large chamber.
Turn to **69**

36

Chili scampers up the side of the tea chest. It smells of old tea and rotting wood. The metal bands that hold it together are poking up to the ceiling in places.

TEST CHILI'S AGILITY with a **DIFFICULTY** of **7**
If you roll 8 or more, then Chili is fine. If you roll 7 or less, he grazes himself on one of the metal straps, and so lose 2 **STAMINA**.
Chili looks into the box. It's mostly empty, but he can see a little packet of something at the bottom of the box.

Do you want him to jump down and investigate? If so, turn to **97**
If you want him to leave the box and look elsewhere in the cellar, turn to **64**

37

Chili falls through the hole into darkness. Despite it being a short fall of only a few feet, he hit his head against the wall as he falls. Lose 4 **STAMINA**.

Then he realises he hasn't landed. He looks around with his keen eyes, and sees that he is suspended a few inches above the floor in a network of fine threads. They glisten in the darkness, and surround his arms, legs and body. Chili tried to kick and fight to get free, but as he does, the threads seem to tighten around him. Then they seem to constrict around him and pull him off the floor, so he can hardly move.

He looks around and sees that he is a few feet into a tunnel. He remembers the hole under the stairs, and realises that this is where he is – he can see a vague light a couple of metres back that must be the entrance from the cellar.

He checks the other way and sees that the tunnel is dark, but what he can see indicates that it is round, but twists, and made of stone that has been polished smooth. More silken threads hang from the roof of the tunnel as it winds its way under Ratpole House.

Then Chili hears a click-click-click-click-click sound. It sounds like many small feet are closing in on him. Turn to **20**

38

Chili goes to pull at both doors. **TEST CHILI'S INTELLIGENCE** to a **DIFFICULTY** of 7.
If you roll 8 or more, turn to **78**
If you roll 7 or less, turn to **65**

39

"Yes", shrieks the garrulous ghoul, somehow able to understand Chili's chirping voice. "*Steeple is indeed my name. I am thrilled, but not surprised, that you have heard of me. I was once, or still am maybe, a famous sorcerer. I lived in this area long before this house was built, long before this fair town was built, when a much older civilisation lived here. But still, even I could not live forever. But still, I live on in my portrait, which somehow found its way here. I must say, Sir Francis has been a most excellent landlord and he even sometimes visits for a chat*"

Chili blinks his eyes slowly, trying to summon the patience to listen to Steeple witter on. He did seem to like to talk, but Chili didn't wish to annoy a sorcerer – even the ghost of one.

"Yes I have much enjoyed my time "living" here, and I have seen you, little fur-ball, around the house – although you may not have seen me. Now, as you have pleased me a little, maybe I can help you a little. I will permit you a question. Think carefully!"

Do you want to ask about?

The gold ring, turn to **9**

The silver necklace, turn to **2**

The copper bracelet, turn to **66**

40

Chili falls back in surprise and nearly falls off the mantelpiece. Then he watches as the face in the portrait seems to expand into the room, as it the man is breaking out of the painting into the real world. But then a figure explodes out of the portrait with a gush of air and the sound of giggles. Chili does topple backwards this time. **TEST HIS AGILITY** with a **DIFFICULTY** of 7. If you roll more than 7, he lands on his feet. If you roll 7 or less, he lands on his neck – and so he loses 2 **STAMINA** points.

Chili looks up and sees a ghostly apparition floating above him. Its face is pale and long, and dark hair floats like a cloud around his head. It's the same face as in the portrait, but instead of looking somber and serious, the face is grinning manically.

"Well, well, what have we here", shrieked the spectre *"it looks like Sir Francis' pet rat has come to visit."* Chili's fur positively bristled with insult from being compared to a rat. The grinning ghost threw back its head and laughed hysterically. It swirls around you, laughing incessantly, seemingly for an age, but eventually regains some of its composure.

"Now Now, little fur-ball, sorry, Professor Fur-Ball! Still, I mean you know harm yet, and may even mean you some well if you can answer me a simple question. Will you accept this challenge?"

If you want Chili to accept this challenge, turn to **15**

If you decide not to risk it, turn to **48**

41

"Oh yes, I know where that bracelet is. There are some strange creatures that seen to have moved in upstairs. They jump up and down and make such a noise it's hard for me to sleep. They really seem to like playing games and sports. When you go up the stairs, don't take the sinister side. I would come with you, but my legs are too tired from running around all night, and so I am staying here to rest."

If that was your first question, turn to **60** and choose another one.
If this was your second question, turn to **25** and choose another option

42

Chili holds his ground, as he is a curious creature (and also a professor and so he does like to learn) and he wants to see what this creature is. Slowly it emerges from the gloom.
The creature is like an unholy amalgamation of a spider, a scorpion and a human. The legs are long and spindly and covered in thick black hairs, like a spider. The torso that rears up out of the legs is like that of a human, although it is covered in thick dark hair. The arms are also humanoid – except of the thick scorpion like pincers where the hands should be.
But the face is the strangest. It's roughly human shaped, but instead of a mouth, there are mandibles that click together. There is no nose, and two sets of eyes. The first pair in the centre are the size of eggs, and multi-faceted like an insects. The second pair are outside of both inner eyes, and smaller. Long, messy black hair covers the scalp of the head. Something gleams from around its neck.

The creature stops, and tiles its head to one side. The **CLICK-CLICK-CLICK** of the feet is replaced by a quieter clack-clack-clack of the mandibles.

Do you want Chili to introduce himself, turn to **79**
Wait for the creature to say something, turn to **58**

43

Chili sat at the front of the house. In front of him is the crooked green door. To the right, round the corner, is the hatch to the cellar. To the left, there is a cracked window (that Mr. March has been asked to fix it as it was letting the house down– but he kept making excuses as he didn't like heights much) on the second floor.

Look at the picture of the house opposite and choose how you want Chili to try to enter the house and turn to that number.

44

Chili skips up the left hand staircase, almost hopping with his back legs, and is soon at the top of the stairs, on the landing. To his right at the other side of the landing is a door, but Chili ignores this.

To his left is a short corridor that ends with another door. Surprisingly, Chili can hear faint singing from behind the door. Luckily its faint, as the singer obviously has a cloth ear.

There is an odd man,
Who maybe lives near you
And if you ever saw him,
Would you even have a clue,
As to what he really is
Let's see if you do
He's tall and spindly,
With a slightly hunched back
With a big bald head
And all dressed in black
His eyes are a staring red
And his teeth long and yellow
He really is,
Quite a strange fellow,
If you ever see him
He may give you a fright
But hopefully you won't,
As he's only out at night

Then the song stops and there is a gurgling noise.

If you want Chili to open the door, turn to **99**

If you would rather he try elsewhere, Chili can either go straight across the landing to another door, turn to **63**

Or Chili can turn to **28** and choose again

45

Chili skips along the landing to the door on the other side. Chili can hear faint singing from behind the door. Luckily its faint, as the singer obviously has a cloth ear.

There is an odd man,
Who maybe lives near you
And if you ever saw him,

Would you even have a clue,
As to what he really is
Let's see if you do
He's tall and spindly,
With a slightly hunched back
With a big bald head
And all dressed in black
His eyes are a staring red
And his teeth long and yellow
He really is,
Quite a strange fellow,
If you ever see him
He may give you a fright
But hopefully you won't,
As he's only out at night

Then the song stops and there is a gurgling noise.
If you want Chili to open the door, turn to **99**
If you have already been here before then lose 1 **TIME** point and then turn to **28** and choose again

46

Chili jumps left through the window to move towards the strange rug on the floor. However, as he does he grazes his left side on a shard of glass that is left in the broken window frame. Lose 1 **STAMINA**
Chili scampers over to the rug in front of the fireplace. The heat from the fire is pleasantly warming, and he is tempted to lie down for a nap. Chili loves a nice nap. But he is instead determined to find Flora's missing treasure.

The rug appears mostly normal, woven from red and blue yarn and with a frayed edge. Chili steps on the bottom of the rug and feels it's thick and warm under Chili's feet, and he curls his toes into the thick wool, and sighs in pleasure. He thinks again if he has time for a nap, but then with regret decides not to. It is not long until morning.

What is slightly strange about the rug is in the top of the rug, closest towards the fire, there appears to be the outline of a silver star in a circle. It shimmers in the firelight, the silver of the star glowing with reds and oranges.

Do you want Chili to step into the circle onto the star? If you do, turn to **94** If you do not, turn to **57** and choose a different option.

47

Chili scampers up the right staircase, taking the steps two at a time. However in his haste he fails to see that one of the stair boards has raised up and he trips. He falls flat on his face. Lose 2 **STAMINA**.

Chili picks himself up and dusts himself down, and takes more care reaching the top of the staircase.
Turn to **63**

48

Chili shakes his head, indicating that he doesn't want to take up the challenge.

"What", shrieks the spectre *"You will not, or dare not even, guess my name? I do not think I like you anymore, you gangrenous rat. Be gone from my home."* With that he waves his arms, his long fingers glow and he points at you. It seems he hasn't lost all of his magical power, as the room around you starts to swirl.

You then find yourself suspended in the air, outside the front door of Ratpole House. Before you have chance to try to open your wings, you fall face first onto the hard stone below. Lose 2 **STAMINA** and 1 **TIME**. You need to find another way in. Turn to **43**

49

Chili scoots up the side of the bike onto the seat, and leans forward and tries to grab the handlebars. Chili is only a small squirrel, about 15 inches tall, and so he finds himself leaning forward, standing on the black seat, and grabbing hold of the handles at full stretch.

As he shifts his weight forward, the bike starts to wobble. It was lent very upright against the tea chest, and as he moves, it starts to tip over to the right side.

Chili can do nothing to stop it, and it starts to falls towards the dirty floor. **TEST CHILI'S AGILITY** with a difficulty of 7. If you roll 8 or more, then Chili manages to jump free. If you roll 7 or less, he falls to the floor and the bike lands on him. Lose 2 **STAMINA** points.
Now turn to **72**

50

It's an almost impossible route, and about halfway along Chili gets stuck solid. There is no space between him and the walls. He can get no purchase on the walls with his claws. He suppresses the instinct to panic, and instead rests and tries to relax.

Eventually his muscles relax and he manages to free himself and crawl along the rest of the tunnel. He then finds himself in the garden of Ratpole House, near the cellar door. However time has run out as he was trapped for too long.
Turn to **33**

51

The walls of the cellar are slick with damp, and the old stones of the foundation walls are so worn with time that they are slippery smooth, and too hard to grip into even with sharp claws. It's going to be a treacherous climb down, even for a green squirrel.

This is going to be a test of how quick and nimble Chili is, and so you will need to **TEST CHILI'S AGILITY**.

The climb requires an **AGILITY** of more than 6.
Roll 2 six sided dice (which will now be called 2d6) and add up the numbers. If you rolled 7 or more, turn to **18**
If you rolled 6 or less, turn to **30**

52

Chili jumps up into the room to move towards the intimidating portrait that hangs above the fireplace. However, as he does he jumps up into a shard of glass that is left in the broken window frame. Lose 2 **STAMINA.** He mutters something to himself in annoyance, but then lopes over towards the portrait. He runs up the side of the fireplace, carefully not to burn himself, and sits on the mantelpiece, staring closely at the portrait. It's of a man, who looks like he is in his mid-40's. He has a long thin face, and his dark hair is swept back from his face, a face that exudes power. It is rumoured, so Sir Francis once said, that the portrait is of a famous sorcerer who lived for many hundreds of years. His eyes seem strangely blank but compelling, so Chili leans in closer to examine them. He blinks a couple of times, and then the eyes blink back at him!
Turn to **40**

53

Chili falls through the hole into darkness. It's only a short fall, a matter of a few feet, and Chili manages to land lightly on his feet.

He looks around with his keen eyes, and sees that suspended from the ceiling around him are a network of fine threads. Chili reaches out a paw and touches one of the strands. It is incredibly sticky and Chili has trouble shaking it from his fur.

He looks around and sees that he is a few feet into a tunnel. He remembers the hole under the stairs, and realises that this is where he is – he can see a vague light a couple of metres back that must be the entrance from the cellar.

He checks the other way and sees that the tunnel is dark, but what he can see indicates that it is round, but twists, and made of stone that has been polished smooth. More silken threads hang from the roof of the tunnel as it winds its way under Ratpole House.

Then Chili hears a click-click-click-click-click sound. It sounds like many small feet are closing in on him. Turn to **89**

54

The star you stepped on is a transport spell, which moves you to another area of Ratpole House, if you know the section for that area.
You find yourself in the catacombs.

Write down **CATACOMBS = 101** as you may need it later.

If you haven't been to this room before, turn to 69 read the text first. If you have been there, then look at the picture opposite **69**, and choose what you want to do next.

55

That's probably a sensible choice. After all, if you were a flying squirrel, you would try to glide down. Wouldn't you?

But it's not that easy. It will take a bit of dexterity to make it down safely, but it shouldn't be too tough a challenge. But **TEST CHILI'S DEXTERITY**
The glide has a **DIFFICULTY** of 5
Roll 2d6 – if you score more than 5, then turn to **74**
If you roll 5 or less, turn to **26**

56

Chili notices that where the bike was propped against the tea chest, there is now what looks like a silver triangle inscribed on the cellar floor. It is protruding out from under the tea chest. It shines quite brightly, even in the dull light of the cellar.

Do you want Chili to try to move the box, to see what the strange triangle is? If so, turn to **70**

If not, return to **24** and choose another option

57

Chili manages to scamper up the wall, his sharp claws finding grip on the mortar between the bricks. It a matter of a few moments he is level with the broken window. The window is divided into four panes, and the one on the bottom right has broken. It has a wide ledge, and he perches on it and peers in. It's a dusty old room that looks like it hasn't been used in decades – or even centuries. Chili has never explored this part of Ratpole as it's rumoured to be haunted. Chili is not scared of ghosts, he just finds them a bit annoying and childish. Look at the picture on the next page and see what you would like Chili to examine when he enters the room.

58

Chili waits patiently until the creature stops before him and looks down at him. It looks down at him.

"Ah, you are the curious creature we have seen recently. You passed through here with some of the humanes, is that not what they are called. We have recently just moved into this lovely dank tunnel. Did Sir Francis not say? But we mean you no harm. We are named Wormald, and we are an Aranesape. We thought you were a ratty at first, a ratty with a silly tail, when we saw you, and we likes to eat rattys, but it seems not"
Chili shakes his head enthusiastically before Wormald could ever think he was a rat. **TEST CHILI'S OBSERVANCE** with a **DIFFICULTY** of 7.
If you roll 8 or more, turn to **27**
If you roll 7 or less, turn to **90**

59

"Ah, Floras silver necklace. I knew I had seen it somewhere before, when I saw them wearing it, but I'll be darned if I could recognise it then. Stupid Maximus. I would have so liked to have retrieved it for her. But if you are looking for it, the current owner lives in darkness in the cellar. And don't speak to them first. I would take you down and introduce you, but I've got some serious chewing to do."

If that was your first question, turn to **60** and choose another one.
If this was your second question, lose 1 **TIME**, turn to **25** and choose another option

60

Chili thinks he recognises the large creature, and reaches up and tugs at one of the long ears he can see. The figure murmurs, and rolls over onto its back, and one of its amber eyes briefly winks open.

It's Mr. March! Or rather Maximus as he is in his wolf form. This may be a stroke of luck, as Mr. March knows a lot about what happens in Ratpole House.

Chili tugs at the ear again, and the great wolf grumbles to itself, but then both eyes flick open and stare at Chili. Maximus roles over again, onto his tummy, and stretches back up, whilst opening his huge maw and yawning noisily and licking his lips. Then he stares down at Chili.
He asks, in his own way, what Chili wants. Maximus and Chili have learned over time to communicate well.

What do you want to ask Maximus about? Maximus likes Chili a lot and so will answer two questions. When you have asked your first one, turn back here to choose again.

The gold ring, turn to **77**

The silver necklace, turn to **59**

The copper bracelet, turn to **41**

61

Chili picks up the round, black bottle. You can just about see that inside are some sort of ground dust. It clings to the side of the bottle and seems to crawl its way up it if. Chili pulls out the cork and the dust rushes out of the bottle and envelops Chili.

This is the Dust of Time, and, and it can increase your **TIME** score. Roll 1d6.

If you roll 1-3, you regain 1 **TIME** point

If you roll 4-6, you regain 2 **TIME** points

Now turn to **25** and choose another option.

62

Chili lifts up one of the doors with a bit of a struggle, as he is only a little squirrel, but being a vampyric squirrel, he is surprisingly strong for his size. The floor of the cellar is about 20 feet below, and all is in darkness. The smell of the room that drifts up is dank and fusty. The door is starting to get heavy and so Chili needs to move. It's too far for Chili to just jump and land without hurting himself.

Should he:

Try to scamper down the wall to the floor, turn to **51**

Try to glide down? He is a flying squirrel after all, turn to **55**

63

The door is closed, but from behind it Chili can hear a lot of sound. High pitch squeals and noises, and the sounds of small feet that seem to be jumping around in the room.

If you want Chili to open the door, turn to **34**

Go straight across the landing to the other door, turn to **45**

Or you can turn to **28** and choose again

64

Chili jumps down nimbly from the top of the tea chest, back onto the cellar floor. Lose 1 **TIME** and turn to **24** and try investigating somewhere else.

65

Chili didn't see the small key in a small lock on one of the doors, and as he pulls it, with the strength he has for a semi vampyric squirrel, he pulls the cabinet towards him as the doors stay closed. It topples down on him, and there is the sound of breaking glass as the bottles inside smash.

Lose **2 STAMINA** points. You wriggle out from under the cabinet and decide to leave it alone. Sir Francis will be furious when he finds out!

Turn to **25** and choose again

66

"Nope, not seen anything like that around here. Anyway, I'm off for a fly around the turrets before sun up. Good luck with your quest"

And with that the spirited spirit floats past you and out of the window. This has been a bit of a waste of Chili's time. Lose 1 **TIME** point.

Turn to **57** and choose something else to do in this room

67

As Chili walks along the dark spaces between the columns, he notices that on one of them is etched a star symbol.

If you want him to continue, turn to **107**

If not, turn to **69** and choose again

68

The mattress is only a few inches thick, and soon all that can be seen in the cellar is the tip of Chili's tail, sticking out of the hole.

Inside, the hole in the mattress leads to a narrow passage that he been burrowed through the wall of the cellar. Chili can see a vague glimpse of light at the end of the tunnel, but this is some way away.

The tunnel keeps getting tighter, and it's harder for Chili to squeeze through it – but he knows that he cannot go backwards now.

TEST CHILI'S DEXTERITY to the **DIFFICULTY** of 10

If you roll 11 or 12, turn to **92**

If you roll 10 or less, turn to **50**

69

The chamber is vast. The floor is a checkerboard of black and white tiles. Reaching up from the floor are several columns that lead up into the gloom. Look at the picture on the next page and decide which way you want Chili to go.

70

Chili pushes the tea chest, and it groans as it slowly slides across the floor. He only needs to move it a couple of feet, and the revealed floor shows that it's now a triangle. It's a 5 sided star surrounded by a silver circle. . Chili gingerly steps across the silver circle and onto the centre of the silver star. It starts to glow brighter and brighter, almost luminously. A number appears at the vertical point of the start. The number is **88**

Write down **CELLAR = 88** as you may need it later.
The room seems to swirl around you and then everything seems to go grey.
If you know the number of a room that you wish to travel to, turn to that number now.
Otherwise, throw 1d6.
If you roll 1 or 2, turn to **85**
If you roll 3 or 4, turn to **80**
If you roll 5 or 6, turn to **101**

71

If you have the Codeword "**TANGLED**" written down, turn to **108** now. Otherwise read on.

Under the stairs to the left of the cellar, there is a dark hole. It's about 4-5 feet high and seems to have been hewn out of the rock, earth and stone under Ratpole House. Chili hasn't seen this hole before, despite being in the cellar recently. He trots over and closely examines it. The earth at the edge of the hole seems quite fresh, as though the hole was only created recently. But by whom?

The hole itself is dark and seems to suck the light out of the room. Even Chili's excellent night vision can see no more than a few feet back. Hanging from the ceiling are thin threads of a silk-like material that gleams in the half-light. A feint breeze emanates from the hole, and smells of rot and mold.

The fur on the back of Chili's neck stands up in worry.
Do you want Chili to enter the tunnel?
If so, turn to **12**
If not, turn to **24** and choose again – but lose 1 **TIME**

72

The bike crashes to the ground, and disturbs the dust on the floor. Chili sneezes twice, as the dust get up his sensitive nose. It may not have been the best idea to try to get a small squirrel to ride a human bike!

TEST CHILI'S OBSERVATION with a **DIFFICULTY** of 9. If you roll 10 or more, then turn to **56**

If not read on

Chili can now either:

Inspect the tea chest, turn to **36**

Or return to page **24** and choose something else to look at in the cellar.

73

Chili has wasted valuable time. Reduce your **TIME** score by 1. Now you must try to get back in again

However, it has also got harder. When you are asked to test Chili, then the scores you will test him again will have increased by 1.

If you want to try:

Through the green door, turn to **14**

Via the cellar door, turn to **19**

Via the broken window, turn to **21**

74

Chili jumps off the door ledge just before the door gets too heavy. He extends his front arms out in front of him, diagonally. At the same time, he extended his rear legs in the same way. The folds of skin between his legs tighten, and he starts to glide to the ground. He steers using his long tail as a rudder, and floats down in elegant spirals.

He lands lightly on the hard stone floor and chitters happily to himself. That was fun!

Turn to **24**

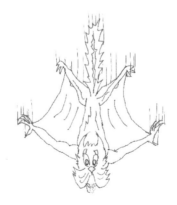

75

If you have the Codeword "**HUNGRY**" written down, turn straight away to **102**

If not read on.

The corridor between the tall pillars becomes increasingly dark and cold. There is a strong smell in the air, an aroma of an animal of some sorts. Chili creeps along on all four feet, increasingly nervous. Then he sees a flickering torch in front of him. He scampers towards it and looks around. Chili slinks into the patch of light and listens. He can hear heavy footsteps echoing through the columns, as something on two feet stomps closer and closer. Then he starts to hear a deep breathing, more like a snorting, as something comes closer.

Then a huge shadow fills the ground in front of Chili. It's the shadow of a powerfully built creature, with horns on its head, carrying some kind of trident.

If you want Chili to stay here, turn to **115**

Otherwise he can scamper back to the main part of the room but you will lose 1 **TIME** point. Turn to **69**

76

Chili picks up the stubby blue bottle and pulls out the cork. Nothing happens. He turns it upside down, and then all of a sudden, a gust of wind seems to pick him up. He is dragged off his feet and something pulls him up into the air. At break neck speed, he flies around the inside of Ratpole, as the gust of wind seems to be able to push or pull doors open at will. Eventually the Zephyr, a mischievous air elemental, drops you in a room. Roll 1d6 to see where Chili has been dumped. However you have lost 2 **TIME** points as you were dragged around Ratpole for some time.

If you rolled 1-2, turn to **57**

If you rolled 3-4, turn to **69**

If you rolled 5-6, turn to **19**

77

"Ah, Chili" says Maximus in his wolven language (which no one would understand if it was written here, and so you will have to take the authors word for it).

"No I haven't seen poor Floras ring. She will be beside herself, poor little rabbit. I would help you find it, but it's time for my next nap."

If that was your first question, turn to **60** and choose another one.

If this was your second question, lose 1 **TIME**, and turn to **25** and choose another option

78

Just before he is about to pull the doors open, Chili notices the small key in a lock on the right hand side door. He turns it and the lock clicks. Then the doors swing open.

Inside are a number of bottles. You must choose one of them, which may help you, or may not.

There is a tall, thin green bottle, with a cork stopper. Chili picks up the tall, slim green bottle and looks at it through the glass. The liquid inside seems to be forever moving, swirling around and around. It almost seems like there are spirits in the liquid, strange faces in miniature that seem to float up to the edge of the glass and then float away. If you want Chili to try this bottle, turn to **11**

Next to it is a short, stubby blue bottle. Inside appears to be some sort of mist which seems to whirl around in a vortex inside the bottle, like a tiny whirlwind. If you want Chili to try this bottle, turn to **76**

Finally, there is a round, black bottle. You can just about see that inside are some sort of ground dust. It clings to the side of the bottle and seems to crawl its way up it if. If you want Chili to try this bottle, turn to **61**

79

Chili opens his mouth and starts to chatter, a high pitched combination of squeaks and chirps. The creature covers the sides of its head with its claws and shrieks in pain. It rears up backwards and one of the legs flicks out, and accidentally catches Chili in the stomach. He is knocked to the floor and grunts in pain. Lose 2 **STAMINA**.
Chili stops squeaking and looks up as the creature looming over him.
Turn to **86**

80

The star you stepped on is a transport spell, which moves you to another area of Ratpole House, if you know the section for that area.
You find yourself in the hallway behind the green door.

Write down **HALLWAY = 80** as you may need it later.

If you haven't been to this room before, read the text first. If you have been there, then look at the picture opposite **28**, and choose what you want to do next.
Turn to **28**

81

The cupboard between the two tall bookshelves looks interesting, and so Chili lopes over to investigate. It's a walnut cabinet, with two doors on the front, each of which has a semi-circular pane of glass. Inside Chili can see two shelves, full of various bottles.
If you want Chili to open the cabinet, turn to **38**
Otherwise, lose 1 **TIME** and turn to **25** and choose again

82

Chili waits a few moments, and when the bracelet is in the air near him, he jumps up and catches it. He lands nimbly at the edge of the mass of Bunions. Chili smiles to himself excitedly as he examines the bracelet, but then he realises the room has gone very quiet. He looks up and sees hundreds of pairs of eyes starting at him, and dozens of mouths snarling, displaying little sharp teeth.

Chili stops, and realises he may have made a mistake. But before he can react, the Bunions are on him, they jump at him, biting with their little teeth.

Chili fights back, but loses hold of the bracelet in the melee. He struggles to get free, and eventually manages to. He turns and runs back to the door, and slams it behind him, panting. He looks down at his body. Fortunately squirrels have thick fur, but even so, there are about a dozen bit marks over his body. Lose 4 **STAMINA** points and 1 **TIME** point.
Stealing the bracelet is obviously not an option. Maybe you can find something that you can swap. The Bunions seem to enjoy games.
Chili can now:
Go straight across the landing to the other door, turn to **45**
Or you can turn to **28** and choose again

83

The creature stops screaming, and then places his head to one side, and bangs on the side facing the ceiling with a long fingered hand. Red liquid pours out of it other ear into the bath. Then it does the same with its other ear, and looks up and smiles cruelly.

"Sorry, Professor, I had something in my ears. I did not mean to shout.", then he picks up a towel and wipes his face clean of the red liquid. The face is light blue and very familiar. "You have caught me at a most inopportune time, Professor," says Sir Francis is a slightly embarrassed tone.

Chili squeaks at him and points at the red liquid.

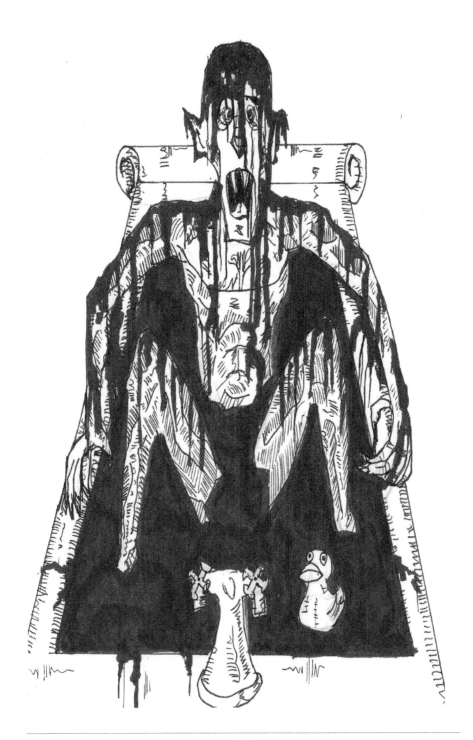

"Blood. No of course not. I have found that a bath just before bed really helps me sleep through the daylight hours. I use some of George's most excellent glood and mix it with the water until it makes a nice consistency. It really is quite relaxing and my skin is so much softer. Would you like to feel?"

Sir Francis sticks out a long stick like arm. Chili shakes his head and takes a step back.

"Ah, maybe not"
Then Chili continues to gesture, and after a few tries Sir Francis works out what he is trying to say.

"Ah the colour. Yes the glood is green, and yet my bath water is red. It is just, and this is sort of embarrassing, I add a bit of food colouring to remind me of the old days when I used to bathe in peasants blood, and this is so much easier. Have you any idea of how many peasants you need to draw a good blood bath?"

Chili shook his head. He didn't, and he didn't want to know.

"I would appreciate if you did not mention this to the children, and Maximus, as they may worry I am reverting back to my old self. Again"

Chili nods his head, but then thinks. He may be able to use this to get some answers out of Sir Francis.

Before we move on, if you rolled and an even number earlier, Chili banged his head on the tiled floor. Lose 2 **STAMINA**.
If you rolled and odd number, he manages to land on his feet unhurt.
Now turn to **91**

84

Chili grumbles to himself as he doesn't like the look of this passageway, but he gets on the ground, front paws in front of him, and stretches his body out behind him. He's now lying face down on the floor. He lifts up his head and crawls, like a soldier, towards the hole.

He measures the width and height of the hole with his whiskers. This is going to be tight. Then he shrugs to himself and crawls into the hole.
Turn to **68**

85

The star you stepped on is a transport spell, which moves you to another area of Ratpole House, if you know the section for that area.
You find yourself in the second floor room.

Write down **SECOND FLOOR BEDROOM = 85** as you may need it later.

If you haven't been to this room before, turn to **57** and read the text first. If you have been there, then look at the picture opposite **57**, and choose what you want to do next.

86

"Oh, we is most sorry" says the creature in a voice that sounds like several voices speaking in unison. *"We did not mean to hurt you, it is just when you sang it hurts our ears. We live underground and are not used to loud noises, especially squeaky ones like yours"*

Despite lying there hurt, Chili felt emotionally hurt as having his voice described as squeaky and puffed himself up.

"We means no insult, it's just the way it is to us. We are sorry"
Chili stands up and dusts himself down and nods his head in appreciation, daring not to speak again.

"We have recently just moved into this lovely dank tunnel. Did Sir Francis not say? We have seen you, yes we have, scampering around. But we mean you no harm. We are named Wormald, and we are an Aranesape. We thought you were a ratty at first, a ratty with a silly tail, when we saw you, and we likes to eat rattys, but it seems not"

Chili shakes his head enthusiastically before Wormald could ever think he was a rat. **TEST CHILI'S OBSERVANCE** with a **DIFFICULTY** of 7.
If you roll 8 or more, turn to **27**
If you roll 7 or less, turn to **90**

87

Chili can do nothing but hang around and wait. But he is also a curious creature (and also a professor and so he does like to learn) and he quite wants to see what this creature is – although he is also a bit scared! Slowly it emerges from the gloom.

The creature is like an unholy amalgamation of a spider, a scorpion and a human. The legs are long and spindly and covered in thick black hairs, like a spider. The torso that rears up out of the legs is like that of a human, although it is covered in thick dark hair. The arms are also humanoid – except the thick scorpion like pincers where the hands should be. But the face is the strangest. It's roughly human shaped, but instead of a mouth, there are mandibles that click together. There is no nose, and two sets of eyes. The first pair in the centre are the size of eggs, and multi-faceted like an insects. The second pair are outside of both inner eyes, and smaller. Long, messy black hair covers the scalp of the head. Something gleams from around its neck.

The creature stops, and tiles its head to one side. The **CLICK-CLICK-CLICK** of the feet is replaced by a quieter clack-clack-clack of the mandibles.

"Hmmm", it grumbles to itself, in a voice that seems to be several voices speaking in unison, *"What are you, you are not a ratty. We thought we had caught a nice plump ratty for our tea, but the rattys we have seen are not green. You have ruined our trap."*

And with that, the creature raises its arm. At the end of the arm is a fearsome claw, like a lobster's claw, with a serrated edge. The creature snips it a few times together in front of Chili's face, and then reaches forward towards Chili.

"We are very sorry, but you have ruined our trap and we must do something about that"

The claw closes in on Chili. There's a **SNIP SNIP SNIP** of the dreadful claw and Chili cries out in pain. Turn to **7**

88

The star you stepped on is a transport spell, which moves you to another area of Ratpole House, if you know the section for that area. You find yourself in the cellar.

Write down **CELLAR = 88** as you may need it later.

If you haven't been to this room before, read the text first. If you have been there, then look at the picture opposite **24**, and choose what you want to do next.

Turn to **24**

89

A shadow appears in the tunnel under Ratpole. It's indistinct as first, as it is small and far away, but soon grows in size. The click-click-click-click gets louder as the figure gets closer, and soon echoes around the chamber. **CLICK-CLICK-CLICK-CLICK-CLICK.**

Chili can start to see a shape appearing in the shadow. First he sees two pairs of multi-faceted eyes gleaming in the shadows. Then the figure is clearer. It almost fills the tunnel, which is about 5 foot tall, and seems to brush past the hanging threads unencumbered. It has a human like torso but instead of hands it seems to have pincers.

The noise is made by its several sets of legs, each of which that ends with a spiked claw.
The face is still mainly in shadow. Apart from the eyes, that shine brightly and with a dreadful desire.
Do you want Chili to turn and run? If so turn to **13**
If you want him to stand his ground and wait, turn to **42**

90

"Anyway, it has been very nice to meet you, but we now have traps to set for rattys if we want to eat tonight. Apologies again that we hurt you."
And with that, Wormald turns around and its mandibles start to chatter together. From the mouth comes long silken threads, which Wormald expertly gathers and sticks to the ceiling, like a spider would create its web. It uses the serrated edges on its claws to snip the threads, as it lays its traps.

It is just as well Chili did not get tangled in the threads or Chili may have been dinner.
Chili turns and leaves the tunnel. Turn back to **24** and choose again

91

Unlike Mr. March, especially when he is in his lupine form, then talking to Sir Francis is much more difficult.

TEST CHILI'S INTELLIGENCE with a **DIFFICULTY** of 6
If you roll 7 or more, turn to **93**
If you roll 6 or less, turn to **17**

92

It's a tough route, and Chili gets stuck a couple of times and gets a few cuts and bruises. Lose 2 **STAMINA**, and reduce your **TIME** score by 2.
However eventually Chili reaches the end of the tunnel, and crawls towards the dim light. He flops out of the exit, and is disappointed to find he is back outside of Ratpole House. He has wasted all that time getting out, and now needs to get back in again!
Turn to **43** and try to get into Ratpole again.

93

Slowly, and rather uncomfortably, as Sir Francis is still sat in the bath naked, Chili gets his points across.

"Ah, so you are seeking Flora's missing loot. A noble quest, Professor. Will I help you? Well I would be honoured. However I cannot in person, as after my bath I have to do my mindfulness exercises and my stretching."

As well as baths, Sir Francis had recently discovered that meditation and stretching relaxed him, especially before bed. And especially after the recent unfortunate incident. He had even tried tantric breathing, but he found that pretty impossible as he doesn't breathe.

Chili looks disheartened, and Sir Francis sees this.

"Do not be concerned, Professor. I have "intel" that may help you on your quest"

Sir Francis has also become a bit too addicted to police shows.
"I know a few things.

Firstly, for the gold ring, know that the current owner has a very sweet tooth, and the stickier the better.

Secondly, the owner of the silver necklace is always complaining that their hair is always matted and sticky. There is a hairbrush over there, take it and maybe they will like this gift"

(Note down that you have a **WOODEN HAIRBRUSH**. Write down the Codeword **TANGLED**)

Thirdly, or finally, or both. The odd creatures who have the bracelet may seem scary, but they scare very easily. Do not be fooled by them. Now that is all I know, and so could you please leave me to my ablutions. And please do not tell the others."

Chili puts his thumb up to say he won't, or tries to. Then he realises he doesn't have an opposable thumb and just nods his head. He turns and leaves the room.
Behind him, the song starts again.
He never ever eats,
So he's as thin as a rake,
And what does he drink?
Well, for Pete's sake
Don't you know by now?
Not water from a spring
Nor milk from a cow
No....Blood is his thing
He'll drink blood from a bat or a rat,
A dog or a horse
A cow or a cat,
Blood from any source
He may even drink
Blood from you
Let's hope

That he never will do
And so if you don't know by now
Let's make it abundantly clear
He is a vampyr
And he has been for many a year
But he was all alone
And really lonely and sad
All the people he's drunk
Are making him feel bad
So he sits all alone
Every evening in his house
All by himself
Well, except the occasional mouse"

To be honest, the lyrics of the song are not much better than the voice singing it. Chili is relieved as he walks away.
You can now ask Chili to either
Go straight across the landing to the other door, turn to **63**
Or you can turn to **28** and choose again

94

Chili gingerly steps across the silver circle and onto the centre of the silver star. It starts to glow brighter and brighter, almost luminously. A number appears at the vertical point of the start. The number is **85**
Write down **SECOND FLOOR ROOM = 85** as you may need it later
The room seems to swirl around you and then everything seems to go grey.

If you know the number of a room that you wish to travel to, turn to that number now.

Otherwise, throw 1d6.
If you roll 1 or 2, turn to **88**
If you roll 3 or 4, turn to **80**
If you roll 5 or 6, turn to **101**

95

The Bunions really seem to like to play games and so maybe Chili has something that they could play with instead of the bangle.
If you have the Codeword "**BOUNCY**" written down, turn to **110**
If not, turn to **103**

96

The star you stepped on is a transport spell, which moves you to another area of Ratpole House, if you know the section for that area.
You find yourself in the cellar.

Write down **CELLAR = 88** as you may need it later.

If you haven't been to this room before, turn to **24** and read the text first. If you have been there, then look at the picture opposite **24**, and choose what you want to do next.

97

Chili hops into the box. It's only a short drop and so he lands lightly on his back legs and sniffs around. His acute sense of smell sniffs out a rich, sweet aroma coming from the corner of the chest. It's the packet he could see from the top of the chest. It an old brown paper bag, the type you may get from a sweet shop.

Chili uses one claw to pull open the bag. Inside are several sweets, wrapped in dark paper. He picks one up and sniffs it. Liquorice!
You have found a **BAG OF LIQUORICE**. Add this to your bag and write down the Codeword **HUNGRY**.
Chili leaves the box. Turn to **24** and choose somewhere else to explore.

98

Chili nears a noise to his left. It's a deep regular and rather loud noise of a large creature seemingly asleep, and snoring its head off. On the upright settee, not immediately visible as it blends into the covers like a fur rug, is a large dog-shaped creature. Its sides raise up and down like a bellows as it breathes in and out deeply.

Chili sneaks over to the slumbering shape. It appears to be either a very large dog, or a wolf, asleep on the settee, snoring loudly.
Do you want Chili to disturb this creature? Maybe you think Chili may know it. If so, turn to **60**
If not, turn to **25** and look elsewhere.

99

Chili reaches up and stretches so he can reach the door knob, and turns it. The door swings inward with a slight squeak.

Behind the door is an old style bathroom, albeit one that had been updated a bit recently. The floors are tiled, as is the wall halfway around. There is a sink against the wall, but no mirror above it (there are no mirrors in Ratpole House). However dominating the centre of the room is a large free standing bath. It is huge, made of white ceramic with silver taps.
The bath is full, but not of water. Instead it is filled with a thick, viscous red liquid. The surface of the liquid is moving and bubbling, as something seems to be under that liquid. Something large.

Chili moves across, and there are steps up to the bath that he climbs, warily. He peeks over the edge, and just as he does, a creature seems to jump out from under that water. It is tall and thin, with a bald head and large pointed ears. The red liquid clings to the creature, and it has its mouth wide open in a terrible grin, revealing long fang like teeth. The creature looks like it is covered in blood.

The creature stares at you with large red eyes, and screams at you "CCCHHHHIIILLLLINNNGGGWOORRTTHHH".

Startled, and scared, Chili squeaks in terror and falls back. Roll 1d6 and remember the number. Turn to **83**

100

CONGRATULATIONS!

Chili has found the gold ring, silver necklace and copper bracelet.

He races over to No.99 and slips back in through the window. He carefully places the items on Flora's bedside table, under her lamp. Chili is exhausted, and crawls into his cage, and falls asleep.

The next thing Chili hears is a squeal. He wakes up, and sees Flora sat up in bed, holding the gold ring, silver necklace and copper bracelet.

"Chili, did you find these?"

Chili nods, still sleepy.

"Oh you wonderful squirrel!" she cries out "Now I can wear them to the party later"

Flora picks up Chili and gives him a tight hug. An hour later, Chili watches out of the window as Flora skips happily on her way to the bus stop with George and Henry

(George is not skipping, as he hasn't completed a health and safety assessment into the dangers of skipping. Henry isn't skipping as he is basically running around like a headless chicken)

With a contented smile, Chili settles down for a nice long nap. It's been a long night!

101

The star you stepped on is a transport spell, which moves you to another area of Ratpole House, if you know the section for that area.
This time, you find yourself in the catacombs. Write down **CATACOMBS = 101** in case you need to travel here again.

If you haven't been to this room before, read the text first. If you have been there, then look at the picture opposite **69**, and choose what you want to do next.

Turn to **69**

102

Chili soon find that path back to where he last saw Morris. He chirps away and soon the tiny tauro appears.

"Ah, Chili, you return. Have you something for me. I am starting to see stars before my eyes – I need something sweet!"
Chili reaches into his sack and pulls out the brown paper bag, and offers it to Morris. He takes it and places it to his nose and sniffs.

"Ah, this smells grand. Liquorice if I am not mistaken. This is a good trade indeed." As he takes a piece and chews on it noisily.
"Delicious. Most excellent, and now a deal is a deal"

With some difficulty, he manages to remove the ring from his nose, and passes it across to Chili. It's covered in snot and so Chili tries to clean it before stowing it away.

Chili bows politely, and Morris casually waves a large hand at him, and turns and walks away.

Write on the **ADVENTURE SHEET** that you now have the **GOLD RING**!

If you now have all 3 items, turn to **100**
If not, turn to **69** and choose where else you want to go.

103

Chili checks his bag but finds nothing that can be of any help. Whilst he is searching, he is aware that the room goes quiet. He looks up and sees that all the Bunions have stopped playing and are staring at him, teeth gnashing.

Should Chili try to stand quietly, if so turn to **109**
Or should he been more aggressive and make himself big like a cat does, turn to **113**

104

Chili examines the candles closely but cannot notice anything else – and in fact he is a bit careless and so he burns his whiskers. Lose 1 **STAMINA** point.

There seems to be nothing else that Chili can currently see, and so he has wasted his time. Lose 1 **TIME** point.
Turn to **28** and choose again

105

Something seems to almost be glimmering under the dirt. Chili brushes the dirt away with his long bushy tail, and sees an image inscribed on the flagstones.

It's a 5 pointed star surrounded with a circle.
If you want Chili to step into it, turn to **112**
If not, turn to **69** and choose again but lose 1 **TIME** point

106

Chili reaches into his sack and pulls out the brown paper bag, and offers it to Morris. He takes it and places it to his nose and sniffs.

"Ah, this smells grand. Liquorice if I am not mistaken. This is a good trade indeed." As he takes a piece and chews on it noisily.

"Delicious. Most excellent, and now a deal is a deal"

With some difficulty, he manages to remove the ring from his nose, and passes it across to Chili. It's covered in snot and so Chili tries to clean it before stowing it away.

Chili bows politely, and Morris casually waves a large hand at him, and turns and walks away.

Write on the **ADVENTURE SHEET** that you now have the **GOLD RING**!
If you now have all 3 items, turn to **100**
If not, turn to **69** and choose where else you want to go.

107

The corridor comes to a dead end. There is nothing in the area, as the floor seems covered in dirt.

TEST CHILI'S OBSERVANCE with a **DIFFICULTY** of 8
If you roll 9 or more, turn to **105**
If you roll 8 or less, Chili gets bored and leaves the area. Turn to **69** and choose again. Lose 1 **TIME**.

108

Having been in the tunnel before, Chili manages to avoid any of the web like threads, and makes his way into along the passageway. He looks and listens and cannot see or hear Wormald, so carefully he reaches up and tugs on one of the threads a few times.

Soon he hears the familiar **CLICK-CLICK-CLICK**

"Oh we hopes we have caught a nice plump ratty." Chili hears the creature mumbling as it closes in on your position. Chili hopes Wormald realises in time that he is not a trapped rat!
The strange creature comes into view once more and stops.
"Oh, it is you again. We had hoped you were a nice ratty for our tea. But have you got something you would like to trade?

Chili reaches into his bag and takes out the **WOODEN HAIRBRUSH** and passes it to Wormald, who seems to quiver with excitement.
"Oh, a brush, it is perfect. Down here it's so hard to stop our poor legs from getting matted, as even sometimes our own threads stick to us. This will help untangle us. Most gratefully received, and now in return...."
Wormald reaches up and, with some difficulty, unhooks the silver necklace from around its neck. A huge claw reaches over, with the necklace handing from it. Nervously, Chili take it and places it in his bag.

And with that, once again Wormald turns around and its mandibles start to chatter together. From the mouth comes long silken threads, as it repairs the slight damage you have done to its traps.

Write that you now have the **SILVER NECKLACE** on your **ADVENTURE SHEET**.

If you have all 3 items turn to **100**
Otherwise, turn to **24** and find a way out!

109

Chili waits a few moments, trying to be non-aggressive.
He watches as the hundreds of pairs of eyes stare at him, and dozens of mouths snarling, displaying little sharp teeth. Chili stops, and realises he may have made a mistake. But before he can react, the Bunions are on him, they jump at him, biting with their little teeth. Then they start to throw him around as if he was a football.

Chili fights back. He struggles to get free, and eventually manages to. He turns and runs back to the door, and slams it behind him, panting. He looks down at his body. Fortunately squirrels have thick fur, but even so, there are about a dozen bit marks over his body. Lose 4 **STAMINA** points and 1 **TIME**.
Chili can now:

Go straight across the landing to the other door, turn to **45**
Or you can turn to **28** and choose again

110

Before going into the room, Chili pulls the deflated beach ball out of his bag. Carefully he inflates it and puts the stopper back in.
He goes through the door and sees that the Bunions are still playing their game. Flora's bracelet continues to fly across the room until another Bunion leaps and catches it. When the bracelet is thrown near Chili, he throws the ball high into the room. The Bunions see it and go berserk, jumping around trying to reach it first as it falls, like a sea of Skittles. The copper bracelet drops to the now empty floor.

Chili pick it up and slips out of the room. The Bunions play on obliviously. Mark that you now have the **COPPER BRACELET** on your **ADVENTURE SHEET**. If you have all 3 items, turn to **100**
If not Chili can now:

Go straight across the landing to the other door, turn to **45**
Or you can turn to **28** and choose again

111

Chili starts to feel dizzy and sleepy, and cannot go on any longer. He finds a corner and goes to sleep. By the time he awakens, it is daybreak, and Flora has already left for school.

Sadly, Chili has not been able to find all 3 of Flora's items in time and she won't be able to wear them for the party.

You can always try again!

112

Chili gingerly steps across the silver circle and onto the centre of the silver star. It starts to glow brighter and brighter, almost luminously. A number appears at the vertical point of the start. The number is **101**

Write down **CATACOMBS = 101** as you may need it later.
The room seems to swirl around you and then everything seems to go grey.
If you know the number of a room that you wish to travel to, turn to that number now.
Otherwise, throw 1d6.
If you roll 1, 2 or 3, turn to **85**
If you roll 3, 4 or 5, turn to **80**

113

Chili makes himself big like a cat. His tail bristles until it's twice its normal size. His fur stands on end. He rears up onto his hind legs and hisses, holding his front paws up in front of him like claws.
The Bunions back away, allowing Chili time to leave the room unharmed.
To get the bracelet he will need to find a toy that will distract them.

Chili can now:
Go straight across the landing to the other door, turn to **45**
Or you can turn to **28** and choose again

114

Ah, a great pity. But if you do happen to find something to eat, then if you return I may be willing to trade the ring. And hurry back, I am starving!"
Write down the Codeword "**HUNGRY**" on your **ADVENTURE SHEET**
However, you have still wasted a bit of time. Lose 1 **TIME** point
If not, turn to **69** and choose where else you want to go.

115

Around the corner comes an impressive figure. Walking upright like a man is a creature with a bulls head, atop a heavily muscled torso. It has two muscular arms, each with three fingers, and held in one hand is a rather wickedly pointed trident. The thick body is covered in dark hair or fur.

Or rather it would be an impressive figure if it were not for the fact it was only just slightly taller than Chili. However, to Chili is still looks pretty scary.

It stomps over to stand over Chili and looks down and says in a not very deep and not very booming voice,

"Harrumph. What is this I see in my lair?" the somewhat-smaller-than-expected Minotaur, asks itself.
Chili starts to squeak an answer, eager to keep this tiny Toro in a good mood.

"It was a rhetorical question, you dolt! Yes I know who you are. You are the former foe of my oh-so-excellent landlord, Sir Francis. I have heard about you from him, but I am surprised that you have never found your way here before. I had heard you were a nosey critter."

Chili feels quite upset by this, as he feels he is more inquisitive than nosey, and he most definitely does not like to be called a critter, but he stays quiet. Then he notices something gold gleaming from the bull-creatures nose. Its Floras gold ring!

"Anyway, here you are now, introduce yourself. It's only polite!"
Chili chitters away and somehow managers to convey his name to the grumpy bull.

"Hmm, Chili, an amusing name. And I must apologise for my briskness earlier. I think my blood sugar levels are low, and that always makes me grouchy. I could do with a snack. Anyway where are my manners? I am Morris, the Minitaur."

Chili looks puzzled and so Morris continues,

"Yes a Minitaur. We are distant cousins to our much larger kin, the Minotaur's. But we have little in common with them apart from a love of mazes. We are not much for eating adventurers, as we tend to have more of a sweet tooth. But enough of that, what finally brings you do my home?"

Chili points and chitters at the gold ring in Morris' nose.

"Ah, you are after my nose ring, but I have grown quite attached to it. If I was in a better mood and no so hungry I may be inclined to let you have it in return. To be honest, nose rings in a bull are so stereotypical and I think I am allergic to the gold, it keeps making me sneeze."

If you have something that you can offer Morris to eat, turn to **106**
If not, turn to **114**

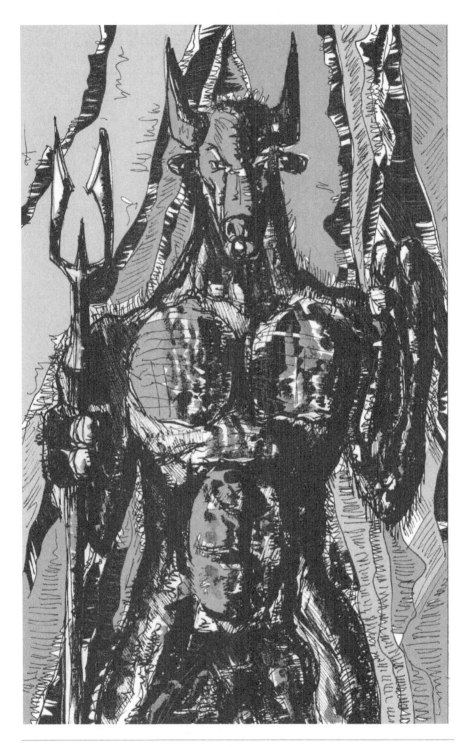

If you liked these cartoons, then please look out for the upcoming book:

Varney the Vampyr: The Cartoons

With over 120 pages of fun with Sir Francis and the gang!